In the Image
and Likeness

Also by Saúl Yurkievich
from Catbird Press

Background Noise

Some other books translated by Cola Franzen

*All Night Movie, The Collapsible Couple,
Dreams of an Abandoned Seducer,
Timorous Women,* and *Mean Woman*
by Alicia Borinsky
Tales from the Cuban Empire by Antonio José Ponte
Horses in the Air and Other Poems by Jorge Guillén
Poems of Arab Andalusia

In the Image and Likeness

By Saúl Yurkievich

translated from the Spanish by

Cola Franzen

CATBIRD PRESS

Spanish originals © 1978, 1982, 1984, 1993, 2003 Saúl Yurkievich
Translation and Translator's Preface © 2003 Cola Franzen
Front cover artwork © 2002 Kurt Schwitters Estate/Artists Rights
    Society (ARS), New York/VG Bild-Kunst, Bonn, Photograph
    ©2002 Museum Associates/LACMA. See Acknowledgments
    for more information.

All rights reserved. No part of this book may be used
or reproduced in any manner without written permission,
except in the context of reviews.

First edition

CATBIRD PRESS
16 Windsor Road, North Haven, CT 06473
800-360-2391, info@catbirdpress.com
www.catbirdpress.com

Our books are distributed by
Independent Publishers Group

Library of Congress Cataloging-in-Publication Data

Yurkievich, Saúl.
  [Selections. English]
  In the image and likeness / by Saúl Yurkievich ; translated from the
Spanish by Cola Franzen.-- 1st ed.
    p. cm.
  ISBN 0-945774-59-1 (trade paperback : alk. paper)
  1. Yurkievich, Saúl--Translations into English. I. Franzen, Cola.
II. Title.
  PQ7798.35.U7A242 2003
  863'.64—dc21
                              2003000260

Acknowledgments

Originals appeared as follows: "Deste colorido sueño" in *Acaso acoso* (Valencia: Pre-textos/Poesía, 1982); "Adorada Duquesa," "Comedia de aparicidos," and "El vagón azul" in *A imagen y semejanza* (Madrid: Anaya & Mario Muchnik, 1993), as well as "El alcance," "Ventura," "La tronquidad," "Algo lo delata," "Pasatiempo," and "El juego del mundo;" "En tus antros," "Veleidoso lector," "Entonces," "A gusto," "Travesía," "Espectáculo," "Historia," "Novela," "Amnesia," and "Correo sentimental" in *Trampantojos* (Madrid: Ediciones Alfaguara, 1986); "Para qué leerlo" and "Espacios" in *Rimbomba*, Pamplona: Poesía Hiperión, I. Peralta, Ediciones, 1978).

Translations appeared as follows: "Novella" in *Reality Studios* (England) vol. 7, nos.1-4, 1985; "Story" in *Temblor* 1, 1985; "Why Bother to Read It" in *Mundus Artium* XIV, no. 2, 1984; "So Then" in *Conjunctions* 9, 1986; "Crossing" in *New Orleans Review*, vol. 14, no. 1, 1987; "Spectacle" in *Pig Iron*, no. 15, 1988; "A Gusto" and "Something Gives Him Away" in *Exquisite Corpse*, vol. 7, nos. 6-9, 1989; "Happiness" in *Rampike* (Ontario, Canada) vol. 7, no. 1; "Pastime" in *Long News* no. 3, 1992; "Trunkiness" in *Intimacy* (England), 1993; "Inside Your Caverns" in *Rampike*, vol. 8, no. 1, 1995. An early version of "About This Painted Dream" appeared in the *Chicago Review* 34:4, 1985; a revised version in *O.ARS/9*, 1993-1994, together with "The Blue Train Car."

The cover artwork, Kurt Schwitters' *Konstruktion für edle Frauen* ("Construction for Noble Ladies, 1919, M.62.22") ("The Blue Train Car"), is held by and appears by permission of the Los Angeles County Museum of Art. It was purchased with funds provided by Mr. and Mrs. Norton Simon, the Junior Arts Council, Mr. and Mrs. Frederick Weisman, Mr. and Mrs. Taft Schreiber, Hans de Schulthess, Mr. and Mrs. Edwin Janss, and Mr. and Mrs. Gifford Phillips.

Regarding the other artworks referred to in FIGURATIONS: *Las meninas* by Velázquez ("About This Painted Dream") is in the Prado Museum, Madrid, and can be viewed on the Web at http://museoprado.mcu.es/prado/html/imeni.html. The portrait of Pareja is in the Metropolitan Museum of Art in New York City, and it can be viewed on the Web at http://www.artchive.com/artchive/V/velazquez/pareja.jpg.html.

The two Majas of Goya ("Adored Duchess") are in the Prado Museum, Madrid, and can be viewed on the Web at http://museoprado.mcu.es/prado/html/imajas.html. The portrait of the Duchess of Alba in white is in the Museo de Alba, Madrid, and can be viewed on the Web at http://goya.unizar.es/InfoGoya/Obra/Catalogo/Pintura/283.html; the Sanlúcar portrait of the Duchess wearing black is in the Museum of the Hispanic Society of America, New York, and can be viewed on the Web at http://www.hispanicsociety.org/english/museum.htm.

Picasso's Suite 347 set of engravings from 1968 ("Comedy of Apparitions") may be seen in Georges Bloch, *Picasso: Catalogue of the Printed Graphic Work: 1966-1969*, vol. 2 (Bern: Kornfeld and Klipstein, 1971). Some can also be seen on the Web at http://www.tamu.edu/mocl/picasso/works (scroll to the bottom of the page and click on 1968).

Contents

Acknowledgments *v*
Translator's Preface *8*

FIGURATIONS
About This Painted Dream 11
Adored Duchess 17
Comedy of Apparitions 39
The Blue Train Car 43

SPECTACLES
Pastime 71
Crossing 74
Why Bother to Read It 75
Happiness 76
Spectacle 78
Inside Your Caverns 82
Spaces 83
So Then 86
The Game of the World 88
Advice Column 92
Something Gives Him Away 94
Novella 95
A Gusto 99
Trunkiness 101
Story 103
The Goal 104
Fickle-Hearted Reader 106
Amnesia 109

Translator's Preface

The prose pieces in this volume are divided into two sections: *Figurations* and *Spectacles*. In the first section, each piece concerns an artist and the creation of certain of their works. In "About This Painted Dream," written in the first person, we overhear Velázquez musing about his painting *Las meninas*. In "Adored Duchess," also written in the first person, Goya, who has just heard of the death of the Duchess of Alba, recounts his intense relationship with her, and the paintings and drawings he did of her. "Comedy of Apparitions" consists of seven sketches in Picasso's series of late erotic drawings. And in "The Blue Train Car" we follow Kurt Schwitters as he assembles the various pieces used in his *Construction for Noble Ladies*. Yurkievich recreates in writing the creation of these works of visual art.

I regard *Figurations* as a major accomplishment. The historical material presented is accurate, and the state of mind of the artists is completely convincing, so convincing to me that when Yurkievich once suggested different wording in "About This Painted Dream," I said, without thinking, that I didn't believe Velázquez would say that.

Yurkievich is uniquely positioned to understand what goes into the creation of a work of visual art. He himself started out as a painter and only later shifted to literature. He is still an active participant in the world of the visual arts; he has collaborated with artists on a number of books and regularly writes essays on art.

The twenty narrations in *Spectacles* are varied in subject and form. Some are very witty, some are serious. Some feature a Chaplinesque character wandering amazed through the world, the world we all have to deal with as best we can. All are, as is usual with Yurkievich, carefully crafted. To turn from page to page is as delightful as twisting a kaleidoscope to discover what pattern the colored bits, the words, will make this time.

It is important to mention Yurkievich's attitude toward language. One of his characteristics is that he uses a wide and varied vocabulary. He will borrow from any discipline that will give him the word with the shape, tone, color, and resonance that fit a particular place. He says he uses "all the vastness of Castilian, except when something is missing," in which case he invents words to fill the gap. His inventions were a challenge: they required that I coin a new word in my language.

Yurkievich's insistence on being as accurate, as precise, as possible, in a medium as slippery as a living language, lends his work both clarity and elegance. His close attention, his deference, to language is a quality the translator can absolutely rely on. This means that the conscientious translator must approach his work in the same spirit.

I found this book a joy to translate; the time and effort required were easily balanced by the delights and discoveries, including in my own language. As usual, I was accompanied line by line by the author, whose help was essential. It was a wonderful voyage. To Saúl, my most grateful thanks.

Figurations

About This Painted Dream

Here at last is my only likeness in which I recognize myself and where I will be recognized. Here is my appearance fixed on this canvas that will survive me. Here is how I see myself, and how I see myself is how I will be seen. Soon, when my heavy flesh ceases to be, they will see the reflection from the mirror of my eyes, the reflection of my world, which my skill, arduously mastered, has stubbornly determined to depict. Here remains my appearance, my apparition to which I give, by means of artful simulacrum, an existence that, although illusory, is more lasting than that of my body, worn out now by so much folly, so much sleeplessness spent adorning naked surfaces with color.

Rival of the sun, with my excessive exertions I have paid for the honors received from this court full of ambushes; caught up in the most diverse duties, I have managed to procure the pleasure of my Señor at the cost of my displeasure. I owe nothing, satisfaction and dissatisfaction balance out, the one his, the other mine.

I paint here, I paint myself in this room of the Alcázar so lavish with paintings. A few years ago it was the seat of his gracious majesty, Baltasar Carlos, whose catafalque it was my lot to design and erect. Oh, sorrowful prince! Various times, thanks to the ingenious tricks of my art, I managed to transfer you to wood or canvas in a manner considered so true to life, although feigned, that now there remains of you, here a boy, here a young man, only the life that my craft gave you, the brilliance of my brush strokes, the bright visions that years ago my brush was able to conceive.

Here I make my portrait, brush in hand, hand at work, given over completely to the task of bringing my image to life, at the cost of my own. I picture myself in this place of certain death, where the reaper snaps the shoots off the tender stalk, in this enclosure of melancholy that causes us to wither, where so many faces grew pale, semblances I had to copy and enhance, this alcove converted from luxurious morgue to a workshop for fabricating depictions that employ the vanity of art to transmute the vainglory of the princes or to balance two illusions: the power of the king with the prominence of the painter that I am, watch the one, mirror the other of this ashen kingdom, of this faded empire of shadows.

"Pareja, mix up for me, quick, a light indigo and a thick crimson. Hurry, Pareja, I have to shade the hoopskirts of María Agustina and make Nicolasito's jerkin more velvety. Then ready for me the carmine, the vermillion, the purple. I have to liven up these brocades that are too austere, make the taffetas flame with scarlet touches. I want to make the fiery red of the water jug rival in splendor the face of the Infanta. The same red reappears on the lower edge of my palette so that the link may be established between them (in the same way light acts as a link making discordances concordances), so that all will know that every aspect these paintings feign with such elegance, all their beauty, are but contrivances forged by my own fantasy."

Such is the clear key to the first enigma, the others are more hidden. This hieroglyphic theater is regulated by subtle symmetries, by geometric perspicacity, that orders, according to distance, the dimensions of forms in the oblique space to such a degree of discipline that the use of visual tricks again becomes a necessity. In the background, the lines of the fallen pyramid converge upon the silhouette of that other Velázquez, a relative who occupies my old post of chamberlain. The vanishing point is situated in the hand of my homonym, who pulls open the veil of forgetfulness to let the light spill out its wonders, to let the light, like the illumination that my art provides, bestow on each distinct object a beautiful existence. And this illustrious hand, allegory for mine, is the same distance away from the one that holds the brush, the one of artifice, as that one is from the tiny angelic hand of the Infanta, a digital triangle that is metaphor for my manual mastery as maker of images.

I am known in the court as taciturn because I do not participate in court society, as biting as it is petty. Aloof from so many intrigues, I prefer saying nothing with my mouth that I can say more eloquently with my images. Words that quicken my inventiveness I find in books that captivate by means of ingenuity and cleverness.

"Pareja, you lazy rascal, no one will give you a more dignified bearing than the one I gave you in my portrait. There you seem as noble as those of good lineage, even more so. In this court of brainless princes anybody is capable of entering the gallery of notables. Look at my jesters and dwarves, my buffoons, my simpletons, they are not merely entertainers; members of the human race like us usually have more common sense than their masters. Pareja, clean these brushes for me very carefully, hand me the sable ones, the very finest. I am missing a yellow, get me a gold and an ivory. I have to lighten the tone of this carpet, where the sun is shining on it. It is furry, the dog is also furry; I will establish a warmer harmony between them."

The same distance as that between the right hands of the two Velázquez, a recurring allusion to the author of such phantasmagoria, the divine face of the Infanta is from the cretinous one of Mari Bárbola, the two of them looking from the scene out at the spectator. Fortune and misfortune have equal billing in the nonsensical theater of this world. Thus, as complementary day and night require one another, so on the proscenium the solar girl and the lunar dwarf are made harmonious. Correlative extremes, with them I provoke at one and the same time a sagacious correspondence and a persuasive counterpoint.

It is presumed that the king and the queen are posing for a portrait of great pomp, and that the mirror in the background duplicates their images. It is understood that whoever observes this painting is placed in the position of the sovereigns; whoever observes it exchanges in a fleeting instant, fugitive as the power of the supreme ones, his low condition for the highest rank. My good King Philip, you who granted me as much glory as drudgery, favors and services are equally matched. Withered majesty of a feeble kingdom, diminished by the war, damaged by misgovernment, I know your face down to the tiniest line; more than thirty times I transfered it to canvas to leave a record of your time, of that wasting away that disillusions and disheartens, of its waxing and of your waning. And the wan queen, the German one, pallid mother of unfortunate progeny, for her I concocted the ceremonial events of her reception, when she came to Madrid for her nuptials; in her honor I erected triumphal arches, arranged majestic perspectives, and raised that Monte Parnaso, where the four continents, over which warring Spain would impose its dominion, celebrate the glory of the imperial bond. Thus the contemptuous sphinx arrived to swell our misfortune. On various occasions I reproduced and copied her, she posing in a sepulchral silence while my brush mimicked the iciness of her masque.

This mirror dims the faces, diminishes; it reflects not so much the face of flesh as that of the soul. The dynastic image is clouded over at the same pace as the empire unravels. The face is as diffuse as the kingdom is dissolute, corruptible, the one and the other, your flesh the same as mine.

"Look, Pareja, I draw everything with this brush. A few traces are enough to make the muslin flowers become full blown, to suggest the pattern of the laces or the diaphanous quality of the tulle. A few skillful touches and the smoothness of the canvas responds, bulges out or forms a hollow; a few appropriate spots let the eye joining them together imagine every material according to its volume and substance, perceive the likeness of each separate thing. And you will ask yourself why this immense, canvas-covered easel is shown from the back, whether the Infanta and her attendants are bursting in to watch me paint the sovereigns or is it the sovereigns who are watching me paint the Infanta. Or perhaps I make believe I paint anyone who rests his eyes on my painting. In one way or another, the easel is the attribute of my craft, a reminder that the pleasures art provides come from this mastery capable of transforming such odds and ends into wonders; it affirms that the marvel consists of paint spread over canvas."

Little breath remains to me, my end is approaching, my body and soul surmise it is so, they divine the departure. I have spent my life fulfilling duties. Finally I paint, for my own account and for my own delight, this allegory, my allegation. Unknown spectator of some tomorrow, remote witness of my talent, to you I leave my alluring labyrinth. I have transmitted the arcanum of my world to the space of this painted dream.

Adored Duchess

They tell me that Cayetana just died, from a bad fever it seems, caused by the Madrid water this stifling summer. She died suddenly, they say, taken by dreadful convulsions as if she had ingested some sort of poison. It wouldn't surprise me if our wily queen had devised some scheme to rid herself of my *maja*. It would have been no problem for her to have one of her minions add the venom surreptitiously to a sorbet or a cool drink such as the duchess used to enjoy. The very tasty one, made of honey and spices, that she used to serve to me herself when I finished my day's work on the frescoes in the Ermita de San Antonio de la Florida. I would take the path from Manzanares to her Moncloa Palace, and there she would be waiting for me to console me in such a lovely way after my efforts, to offer me not a little solace. María Luisa is capable of any evil. She, more than anyone, hated and envied Cayetana for her more ancient lineage and her bearing, infinitely finer and more elegant than that of the dumpy matron who rules over us. And all Madrid knew how they fought over the handsome Pignatelli, who never learned to maneuver, as he should have, between two rivals ready for anything. Indulged by the two most powerful ladies of the court, he grew conceited and unaware that he was in the line of fire; he only saw himself showered with luxuries. A double offensive of repudiation caused his undoing, but only fleeting, I think. How well I know these high and mighty men. Such fickle types manage never to fall too far from their peak; they suffer only temporary disaffection and exile. I know these people who keep me in a servile capacity at their bidding, sleazy characters who praise me and humiliate me in equal measure.

Everybody in the Court knew that the then princess, full of mistrust and jealousy, watched Cayetana with all her perverse soul, because Godoy, her favorite, was smitten like so many others by my duchess, was involved in a fling with her, with the duchess of Alba. María Luisa was unrelenting until she obtained the crown and could claim Godoy for herself, though never entirely. But Cayetana could subdue and hold anyone she fancied for as long as her infatuation lasted. It happened that way with me, first because of my painting. I was already highly regarded in the court. The most enlightened ladies, those of noblest ancestry, requested that I make their portraits. That's how I came to paint the duchess of Osuna, with such skill that she promptly asked me to decorate the great hall of Capricho according to my own ideas. Cayetana was a frequent visitor, a member of the circle that the duchess of Osuna gathered around her in the Alameda Palace. There it was that she first saw and was attracted to my country scenes; from the beginning I wished to include her among the various personages pictured in them. About that time I also did a portrait of the elegant and arrogant countess of Carpio, as skinny as a mendicant monk, the opposite of my charming and vibrant duchess of Alba. As for the countess of Carpio, I had no choice but to dress her in black. She is the one who should be occupying the throne; she has the presence and distinction of a monarch, entirely different from the plump, coarse one we have. As for the queen, I did my best to improve her appearance in my portraits, but without sacrificing vigor and veracity. Somehow, though, my contempt comes through.

Damn this spiteful court, more a cohort of depraved wastrels, damn the ones devoid of all decency who seek me out so that I will perpetuate them on my canvases. And the ninnies boast of my portraits, where I paint them exactly as they are, their mugs and ilk, ugly and fatuous. That way at least I leave to posterity my testimony of the royal breed that misgoverns us. How could my madcap duchess, so smart and so sharp, become enamored of that hypocritical lightweight, that conniving, presumptuous Godoy, who takes advantage of everybody and was bound to use her too for his rapacious ambition? Perhaps her interest in him was nothing more than a whim and, later, defiance, to annoy and humiliate María Luisa, now risen to the rank of queen but lacking the prestige of the Albas. How could Cayetana fall in love with that treacherous fox Godoy, who brazenly deceives the delicious, delicate María Teresa? If only María Teresa's father, and my friend, the Infante Don Luis, had not left her an orphan at such an early age! He would never have done anything so senseless as to plunge her into misery by marrying her off to Godoy. A lovely child she was, like her mother, the Zaragozan Infanta of Vallabriga, whom I knew well and who showed me much appreciation. With complete pleasure on my part and with all my skill at her service, I painted her, whenever she asked me, in her room and on horseback. The daughter, as versed as her mother was in the subtlety of art, respects me as well. I painted her recently, and also when she was a little girl, in her exquisite tenderness, looking straight at me, watching how I copy the world with my brushes, there in the large portrait of the Infante's family, the one in Arenas de San Pedro. Not long ago, I made my favorite portrait of her, now married and early in her pregnancy. Here I show her in her sad sweetness, the unloved little countess of Chinchón, my pretty one, the light blue of her dress complementing so well her smooth pale skin. And over the spilling curls of her hair, gold tending toward copper, I placed a spray of green shoots to celebrate the yet unripe fruit of her womb. I made sure that the dignity proper to her would emanate from her figure, trying in my fashion to protect her against Godoy's outrageous behavior. Even in María Teresa's presence, he shamelessly divides his attentions between the vivacious Pepita Tudó and the vulgar María Luisa. The little countess of Chinchón has little in common with you, Cayetana, except perhaps with your fondness for painting and for the court of swindlers that draws both of you into its schemes, making both of you targets of that pair of tricksters, the queen and her favorite. You were more of a child than the little countess when you were given in marriage to the affable Marquis de Villafranca, who served more as protector than as voluptuous lover, able to calm your ardent temperament.

There is no greater fortune for a painter than to be both loved and understood by those who request his art, just as it was for me with the Infante and his splendid wife. Never before had I felt so contented as in his palace of Las Arenas de San Pedro, when I made that immense canvas of the family of Don Luis. Through the felicitous imagery of that painting, I tried to give a true reflection of the happiness that during my stay there enveloped us all. While I stayed with them, they all showered me with the most affectionate, heart-warming attention and admiring flattery. I believe I was correct to show them in their everyday intimacy, the room lit only by a candle, which accentuates the chiaroscuro and brings out the great dignity of the silhouetted figures posing against a shadowy background. They seem to emerge from the darkness as if from the depths of my memory, just as my fancy convokes and disposes them, with myself the portrayer willingly appearing alongside the portrayals of my beloved ones. In the very center I placed María Teresa, mother of the little countess, wearing a white muslin robe; her hair, a radiant triangle that ends in that beatific countenance, is being arranged. And Don Luis, who is amusing himself with a game of cards, I put him in sharp profile, as on a medallion. I am with them, my back to the spectator, down in the left corner, leaning over the canvas, mahlstick, palette, and brushes in hand, engrossed in the exercise of my skill, like that Don Diego whom I admire so much and emulate, and whose mastery I believe I come close to in this canvas.

You, too, Cayetana, I portrayed you with your talisman, your little Pekinese dog. No man, in my opinion, was ever so petted or loved by you with so much constancy as your adored Pekinese. In that painting, devoted wholly to you, I put at your service, as never before, twice over, my proclivity and proficiency, the love that you inspired in me and all my craft. Already when I was working for your friend María Josefa, of Osuna, you told her that you were keeping a sharp eye on her because she was monopolizing me. Already then, in the gatherings at her quinta de la Alameda, where many illustrious people came—Quintana, Iriarte,

Menéndez Valdés, Jovellanos, to mention the closest of friends—you gave me signs of such esteem that you kept my heart aflame as nobody had ever been able to do. Added to your praises was your keen eye, eye of an infallible tester, sure to discern what truly matters in painting. For all that, for your good taste, you delighted in owning, among other marvels, the admirable Venus of Velázquez, the only, the one with the mirror. And ever since I saw you, thinking of your pleasure, I cherished the idea of painting your beauty, painting you—what cupidity!—like that Venus who accompanied you in all her resplendent nudity. I painted you with my ardor and art given over to your loveliness. And to make you stand out, I put in that background of field and sky, which other ladies, to imitate you, would later ask for. Whatever you did, other women would copy right away, such as your way of dressing like a *maja*. Already then, I knew that you responded to my compliments, were pleased by my devotion, and this led me to incorporate in your portrait the ruse that discreetly joins us, the forefinger of your right hand pointing toward my dedication, written at your feet. In this slanderous world, how else could I depict you in a portrait worthy of your rank and requested by your good husband? Only as a painter who takes account of your slenderness and grace, the charming vitality of your figure, heightened, I believe, by those red ribbons, like flames on the sheer chiffon of your dress, which alludes to the sensual and fiery side of your character. Here, my sorceress, you are as I admired you, with your slim waist, full breasts, long straight throat, the jet of your large eyes and the black black silk of your forest of curly hair.

So much, so great was the difference of lineage and fortune between your family and mine that despite the recognition the grandees of this kingdom granted to my art, I did not dare give full rein to the powerful affection I felt for you right from the beginning. I knew—who didn't?—of your amorous entanglements, your love affairs with the gallants of the moment, your lascivious appetite which nobody managed to sate. No one seemed born or skilled enough to hold you. What could a painter expect in the way of passion: in his fifties, half deaf and somewhat ugly, often laid flat by illness, with a burdensome family to care for, always angling for the sops that the frivolous, coarse, and dissipated characters might choose to toss his way? Nevertheless, just as everything about you turned out to be surprising, you responded, perhaps out of mere caprice. Just as you fell in love with bullfighters, skilled in an art as polished as mine, you responded to my love. Since you were so attracted to bullfighters, I induced you to take an interest in the corridas, I taught you about rules and strategems, the feints and flourishes of tauromachy. I saw you were taken with the Romeros; first with Pedro, the oldest and best known, then with his brother José, both extraordinary in the ring. I, as expert with my brush as they with their passes, had the pleasure of portraying these two Sevillians; I was able to bring out both their elegance and their precision. You were captivated by men whose power did not depend on possessions and titles. You admired my ability to recreate you on canvas with all the allure you exhibited in living flesh. I find no other reason for my influence, given the few good looks granted me by fortune, with my grim face like a bull and the countenance of an irascible bulldog. I suppose that, in your eyes, I had the ardor and vigor I put into the best of my works; you appreciated my zeal, so easily stirred up, that spirit your presence gave back to me. How could I resist you when you turned my ferocity into renascent rapture? With you, my cares were eased, I recovered my mettle, the blood strained in my chest once again; you restored my appetite for living, you returned me to the prime of life.

When you were widowed, you felt freed of the matrimonial ballast, even though you had been able to count on the indulgence of the Duke, who had married you when you were thirteen years old and he only a little older. To avoid the strictures of mourning, you decided to take refuge in your estate at Sanlúcar. To my great delight, you took me with you, together with the amusing members of your entourage. You made it possible for me to enjoy the happiest time I ever savored in my existence of toils and tasks. My pleasure was barely mitigated by that famous mishap of your coach on the slope of Despeñaperros. It was, as its name warns—Dogsprecipice—a proper place for adversity. That accident cost me an entire night of exhausting work in frigid weather. With utmost effort I managed to repair the axle which we had to straighten by heating it in a bonfire of logs. The chest cold I caught thanks to the chill morning air certainly aggravated my deafness. But everything in Sanlúcar turned out to be extraordinary; your spontaneous gaity was contagious, the air limpid and warm, your beauty radiant as the light of those places whose summer splendor matched yours exactly. Spurred on by you, I enjoyed you, and both of us succumbed to amorous straying.

The combination of these delights produced an avalanche of wonders. All my senses found their proper gratification at your estate of Doñana. I rambled in ecstasy through the manor house, saw how the light streaming in harmonized with forms and colors, how in the kitchen its chiaroscuro matched the dishes and provisions. A thousand scenes, a thousand possible still-lifes invited me to paint them. I wandered through your quarters to contemplate you when you were at your leisure or preoccupied. I watched as you dressed yourself up, changed your attire, now in light clothes, now all bedecked, in a *maja* outfit like your beautiful maids, bantering and gossiping with your attendants, teasing and scolding your old *dueña*, so pious, or amusing yourself with your pampered page Luisito Berganza and with your little black girl, the charming María de la Luz. I remember you, your breast uncovered, pretending to nurse her. I walked through all the outbuildings, delighted in observing your servants busy with daily duties. I went from garden to orchard, enraptured by the odors of jasmine, carnation, and oleander. Everything was alive, in constant motion, always coupled with such jubilation that I decided to fix on paper at least something of the abundance of the most pleasurable things that went on around me. The best way for me to relate to the people and things that stirred my spirit was to translate them into images of my own making. In the heaven where you are now, do you remember that sketchbook of long ago, the one I bought in Cádiz and kept filling with washes, almost all devoted to you? I had to get my eye and hand accustomed to capturing quickly and with few strokes those special but furtive moments. It was essential that the people there accept my indiscreet presence and let themselves be sketched by that curious man who stalked them at every turn, paper in hand. They all asked to see my drawings, and were pleased when they looked and recognized themselves. You never knew how much my art owes to those exercises of sure quickness. It was in Sanlúcar, under your tutelage, that I gained my singular mastery of drawing. There I was finally able to record whatever went on around me, to capture what lives and moves without immobilizing it. I acquired the sharpness needed to get down directly, with agile pencil or nimble brush, whatever the eye is seeing, to make a vivid summary of the most salient features. Although bedazzled, I glimpsed all the possibilities offered by this method. I felt that I could bring the whole world into my art, chronicle its endless variety, instruct or give reign to fancy, as I tried to do soon after in my Caprichos. You were always asking me for the album, to see yourself just as I caught you, foreshortened, stretched out on your bed, on your back, nude, looking at yourself in the mirror, where your face is reflected, or throwing your head back with your hands in the tangle of your hair. You were so amused by the sheet where on the front you are standing wearing a dress with ruffles, and on the back you are looking at me with a devilish expression as you lift your skirt to show me your glorious behind.

And to reveal your beauty and extol it, I offered you my rapturous tribute: the Sanlúcar portrait, larger and more powerful than the one done for your late husband. I was no longer hampered by circumspection, as I was when you were married; there was no reputation to safeguard, I could glorify you in my painting without pretense. That is why you are here, so radiant, as you were in life, with all your charms smug, impudent, as if to provoke the audacity of anyone who admires you. Your black skirt and lace mantilla are not signs of eloquent mourning but of elegant splendor. The black enhances the yellow of your *manola* jacket—your pose is that of a *manola*—and it heightens the red of your sash, its gold flecks revealed by the lace. The fabrics let me play with materials and their particular qualities, something I enjoy. All that very sumptuous black serves to adorn you and make your silhouette stand out from the receding landscape; black is the lace puffed out by your dark hair, and black your intense eyes. I treated the attire and coiffure with rapid and vigorous brush strokes, in order to concentrate with special care on the uncovered part of your flesh, your face and your right hand. I worked on the hand like a miniaturist, painting all the details, above all the two rings. A close observer can read on one Alba and on the other Goya, inscriptions meant to seal a union that will remain on the canvas even though in life it might be transitory. As in the Madrid painting, you point with your index finger to my signature written in the sand so that only you can see it: *Sólo Goya*, the deluded one who wished in vain to keep you.

From Sanlúcar we went back to Madrid, with your retinue, to your palace of Moncloa. In seclusion there you saved yourself from the harassment and gossipmongers at court. You found dressing in mourning tiresome, and so you walked through the gardens with the ladies of your company, all of you decked out as winsome *majas*, wearing lace, low-cut necklines, and bolero jackets and high combs like the graceful girls who stroll seductively through the Prado in search of some fellow to fleece. I stayed by your side like a devoted lackey, hungrily begging for the crumbs of your love. I kept accumulating pages of sketches to preserve some trace of that happiness. I presumed that soon you would start to stint on your attentions to me.

I came to feel an immense liking for your figure, it was so imprinted on my brain, it shaped my manner of working to such a degree that every time I draw a girl, your image prevails. That's why in the Caprichos your bearing and your elegance reappear everywhere, whenever women of handsome appearance are seen. Every *maja* in the Caprichos, strutting, enthralling, ensnaring, plotting with witches, bawds, and pimps, flaunts your semblance, shows how you have entangled me in your whims, how much your crazy behavior has harmed me. Every time an attractive woman appears in my Caprichos, she resembles you. There is much of you in every pretty lady, no matter what her status. As if hinting at your approaching death, that lovely *manola* with her lace dress looking at herself in the mirror, in which she sees a caduceus of the Reaper and serpent, is you. So it might be known, I added, as symbol of your flightiness, the butterfly, seldom still, never at rest. It is you pulling on a stocking in the presence of her procuress; the one holding up the garter; the bedecked one who, walking by, seeks to arouse desire—those who pay may enjoy her; that one plotting shady deals with members of her crafty cabal; the one who uses her love as barter; the fickle one; the frivolous one, the one so enamored of flitting about. All represent you. The one who spreads her mantilla to take flight and is held up in the air by crouching witches, like monstrous caryatids—that one also is you, Duchess. Like the Virgin carried by the angels in Assumption, you ascend thanks to your lightness, raised above the dais of Beelzebubs, site of grotesque sorcery. But most of all, you are the one with two heads, the one in my dream of lies and inconstancy, an obvious reproach for your fickleness, such a clear reproof of your duplicity that, satisfied with engraving and pulling that print, I did not include it in the Caprichos. How could I make it public, cause a scandal I could never get used to, for anyone would have been able to recognize us; me, the submissive and gulled lover embraced and kissed by the provocative beauty, and my Cayetana with two faces, one showing me her affection, beguiling me, the other turned toward her cohort, a procuress, also with a double visage, who has just arranged a traitorous encounter with the youth whose hand clasps that of the capricious one. Thus content, the young rogue enjoys beforehand the imminent tryst. As headdress you wear two butterfly wings, one for your infidelity, the other for your falseness. And to create the atmosphere for my anathema, I gave free rein to my fantasy, to those lugubrious chimeras that propagate in my dreams and in my Caprichos. Meanwhile, here crouching at your feet, in order to cover up the chicanery, Lucifer's envoys veil that loathsome witch with sacks for arms and the serpent hypnotizing the frog in order to gulp it down. My suffering bulldog mug is plain to see, my snub nose and my protruding lip; your caress appeases me even though I may not know that I am sole possessor of your mercurial love.

In shameless Madrid, back to the licentious, mischief-making court, caught up in revelry with fops, you returned to your old tricks. And I, with the scorpion of jealousy gnawing my entrails, humiliated by having to contend for you with dissolutes and profligates, shared you with dandies and bullfighters, with the chorus of gallants. You returned and were soon ensnared in the ruses of that bungler Godoy, who, to crown my chagrin, never stopped praising me or soliciting my services as painter, probably at your instigation. I had no other escape from the unwelcome business of this world, from the sorry bondage the court imposed on me with its demands, than to take refuge in my fabulous figurations, my capricious extravaganzas. To them I devoted every moment rescued from my official duties. To top it off, I was overwhelmed by troubles, my deafness was growing worse, my health declining more and more, in the hands of asinine and harmful doctors who rather than make me better robbed me of both life and funds. And all my clients wanted ceremonial portraits that would glorify them in immense, magnificent images. How many asked me, all at once, for equestrian portraits, such as the veteran garde de corps of María Luisa, the silly Godoy, eager to emulate the sovereigns? The queen was so completely satisfied with my portraits that she had me named first court painter. Above all she was delighted with the picture where she stands wearing a black lace dress, an exquisite mantilla—a custom she imposed on the court against the French style preferred by some—and silk, gold-embroidered slippers. I did what I could to bestow on that stocky body and coarse face a certain fineness. Very proud of her bulgy arms, she insisted that I paint them uncovered. I took great pains to endow them with a delicate roundness, accentuating the one that rests on her thigh with porcelain reflections. The dark clothing makes her chest and rosy face stand out, the contour clearly outlined in contrast to the aquarelle landscape of the background.

Such honors, the greatest to which a craftsman can aspire, were late in coming to me; I had coveted them, but my ill health and setbacks made them meaningless. I had built up too great an aversion to the powerful, as well as indignation for how they totally ignored the misery of ordinary people. Seeing the multitude of needy teeming in the streets of Madrid, crushed and groaning under the load of hunger and helplessness, I could not tolerate the squandering of that misbegotten nobility, as avid for luxury as they were obtuse. The empty vanity of the rich was utterly repugnant to me, all the more unbearable because I was dependent on them, on their damned commissions that took up all my time and sucked my brains dry. I wanted to use my art to satisfy other disquiets, other aims than just to portray in servile fashion our contemptible rulers. My own visions occupied my mind and urgently besieged me. I rushed to put them on paper or canvas. I felt the call of other worlds than that of the court, and could not manage to reconcile such different demands. The less I wanted to be linked to the pomp of the kingdom, the more they shackled me with official requests. You yourself gave me the key to my contradictory situation. Like nobody else, perhaps without wishing to, without malice, you brought to light my inner quarrel. Never will I forget that evening when you burst noisily into my new studio on Valverde. Godoy the favorite had bought my other house from me, the one on Desengaño, Disenchantment Street, a name that better suited my condition. There he installed his long-time mistress, Pepita Tudó, and then asked me to make the portrait of his wife, the little countess of Chinchón. You appeared suddenly amid a lot of clamor to ask me to paint your face. You simply dropped into my studio and got what you wanted. I was working away, calmly preparing an outline for the portrait of the duke of Alcudio on horseback, when you demanded that I make up your face for some party. Since I was a dauber who daubed great dames to improve their features, how could I refuse, you said to me, to beautify the one dearest to my heart? At first I was unnerved by how brazen was your wish to take advantage of my craft for the adornment of your face; finally, I understood that you were right, that I was an inflated lackey at the service of the highborn and the bigshots, and that among those grandees of Spain there you too were, my adored Duchess. How then, if I am a mere hireling, painter of scarecrows and of masks, bedizener of hobgoblins disguised as gentlemen and bogeymen dressed like kings, how not paint you, directly over the smoothness of your skin, who better than I to dispose the colors over your countenance, to heighten your exquisite beauty? I gave in as usual to your vagaries.

It was midsummer, I remember, around August of 1800. The sun's glare came burning through the large windows, lighting up your face. I preferred to color it, on you, than to paint it on canvas. Using your cosmetics, to which I added some of my pigments, I powdered you very lightly, to avoid the look of a mask, spread over the smooth tenderness of your cheeks a pale pink, shading it as it went away from the cheekbones, put some touches of brighter pink beneath the eyebrows, to accent the jet black of your eyes, evened and marked with charcoal your eyebrows' arch. With a fine sable brush I applied crimson over your thin lips, following their natural contour. What nature had delineated so skillfully did not need my corrections. I harmonized the pinks to match the gradations of your lively skin, followed the delicate undulations, the progressive passages from the hollow to the protuberant, working within a similar, shaded range, toning down any contrast so that everything might be shown as it was, enhancing each part in its own appearance, in the grace of its properties, so that the proper splendor might be more evident, its charm more manifest, so that she might look more like herself than ever, more like her very inmost self. While I caressed her face, I said to myself that I would not stop painting her, that I would not give up until I had painted her whole, that I would paint her whenever and however she appeared, no matter the manner and moment of her coming. To paint her body, that is what I craved, to paint her entirely, dressed for any occasion, and finally nude, for me, so that I might idolize her, fix her, brought to life and perpetuated by the hand that touches you, glorified by me in your most intimate fullness, María del Pilar Teresa Cayetana, my duchess of Alba.

To think that they buried you at night almost without any obsequies, so that nobody would see your body dried out by fever and consumed by vomiting, nor your face disfigured by death throes. While I painted your face in that August of the year before last, I joked with you, saying that if I made up the face, why stop at the neck, that since I was in the midst of the task I could beautify your entire body. It was then that you announced that you had me in mind for a similar undertaking. You were passionately involved in building and decorating your new palace of Buenavista. You were devoting all your attention and a good part of your fortune to that lavish dream. You wanted to outdo all your peers, even the grandest, in elegance and splendor. Your ambition was to erect in the Huerta del Corregidor a residence appropriate to your taste and rank, to show the rustic nobility of Spain how provincial they had become, how backward they still were. There, according to what you told me, you had set aside a private room especially prepared to receive your most loved paintings. To crown the collection, you wanted me to make two full-length portraits of you, both oblong, one dressed as a *maja* and the other in the same pose, but nude. You demanded that nobody know of them, warned me that they would come for me, that I would be given lodging in your house and kept there as long as the painting went on. It happened just as you foresaw. You locked me in to make sure that I would devote myself entirely to that delicate, delicious labor. Right away, you offered to pose and I started to make sketches, to arrange the setting most pleasing to us both. I chose the divan of greenish plush, where you were to recline on the large pillows with ruffles, then we agreed on the position that would allow your body to be seen from the most favorable angle. We also decided on your costume: the golden bolero with black bobbin lace, sheer white dress, and a red sash tight around the waist. Then, when I was drawing you with the brush and with great enthusiasm preparing to mold the volumes, you demanded that I change the face so that no one could recognize you. Suddenly you had lost your nerve and, reconsidering the challenge, retreated. You preferred that Mariantonia pose for me, your closest attendant, well disposed to be the alternative, an appetizing girl no doubt, but more hefty, with breasts and belly more rounded than yours. That is why I revealed them so provocatively beneath the dress that clings to the torso and legs and faithfully shapes to the feminine curvature of her body. I made that Maja with enjoyable ease, using quick brush strokes, my sketching style, so that the verve of the coloring would prevail, so that something of your presence would vibrate in it. When I painted her nude, you are the one who was in my mind. Although you no longer posed, you are the one I painted. Not with your features nor with your build, but with a similar beauty, with all your charm, with the sum of delights that belong to you, with that body I always yearned for, your personal essence. I again painted you, in the same pose, with your hands behind your neck, settled like Titian's Venus, which you own, so that the creases and furrows of the belly are attenuated, the undulations softened. I finally painted you the way I longed to, unclothed, in your most intimate truth, in your offering to me of your nudity. With my brush I caressed you all over, with my colored paste fashioning that other tenderness, your nacreous roundness. And the brushstrokes of light pink tints with which I approached the intimacy of your flesh were my license: the possession of your figure by the thief's gaze.

Incited by the delight of your body, which I relished as I looked at it, I sought to take account of the tenuous passages of light to shadow, managed to make the qualities of your warm skin bloom from the impasto, as if painting and touching were the same certainty, the same evidence. Possessed by that tempting body, I fought to bring over not only tints and tones, but also the illusion of consistency of each part. Meanwhile, I could not stop thinking about your Venus of the mirror. You told me you would hang my Majas in the same room with it. To be placed next to the most magnificent of painters, the greatest Spaniard that ever was, intimidated me. I told myself that I, the admiring emulator, would dare, in a century of mediocre talents, to come doubly close to that insuperable master. On the one hand, I took up under his aegis the almost abandoned theme of the female nude (damn my hypocritical colleagues who let themselves be intimidated by prudish priests!) and, on the other hand, I had the honor of having my work exhibited by your side, brilliant Velázquez. For a painter there is no more tempting material than flesh. Of changeable color, rather undefined, neither white nor pink, of a special texture, in its own way it absorbs light as it reflects it. Thin and thick, swollen and tight, it presents arduous difficulty to the artist who must reveal its mystery on an indifferent canvas. At last, by my art, you were made plainly manifest. Although I had to superimpose different features over yours—somewhat perturbing the accord that nature herself had composed—you remain there forever in your prime; there you are at leisure showing your gifts without concealment, lithe, licentious, unashamed, like a goddess.

Shortly after finishing the Majas, the earlier false count and now novice prince, the omnipresent Godoy, searched for me insistently, urged on I think by my friend Meléndez. He and Jovellanos were both fooled by Godoy, who passed himself off as enlightened. Although they were upright magistrates, they were bad judges of Godoy and did not discern his true nature. Men of great learning, fair in the censure of errors and vices, they did not perceive how he played up to them to suit his momentary interests, or that he could abruptly switch his allegiance according to circumstances. The arrogant upstart celebrated my art more and more, showed me growing esteem, and even took me out in his grand carriage, so comfortable that during the ride we could enjoy refreshments. More than his military merits, it was the orange groves of Olivenza that earned him the rank of generalissimo in our ludicrous war with Portugal. To celebrate his victory, he arranged that I be chosen to paint his official portrait, as a special mandate from the Kingdom. I had no choice but to comply, despite my jealousy, which went hand in hand with my abhorrence of him. Forced by his power, constrained by my position as first court painter, I undertook that commemorative portrait, although I am appalled by anything warlike. Nothing is more disastrous for the life of common people than war. It is worthwhile, I gave myself the excuse, to make clear the character of the individual who has achieved great eminence so quickly, such is my mission as a painter of my time. On that canvas, almost three meters wide, Godoy is seen installed in triumph on a large sofa, as if on a throne. The battle over, its clangor suggested by a stormy sky, Godoy poses naturally, his body leaning over his bent arm, dressed with greatest pomp, as though for a court ball, with the insignia of generalissimo clearly visible on his chest. Two captured enemy flags symbolize the conquest. Although it is a celebratory work, the figure shows him just as he is, young and vigorous, the Godoy who rules the destiny of Spain, who still has access to your chambers. He knows my Majas; you showed them to him with impudent arrogance, I have no doubt, and he covets them already, because he finds them exciting and because he is not without taste in questions of art. I do not trust him to be discreet. He surely told the Queen that I painted you nude and later had to change the face. Now, like a lightning bolt that strikes with full fury in the chest, they bring me the news of your sudden death. I fear that he will take advantage of his privileged position to get hold of your treasures, to rob you of your Majas. I know him, I know his lascivity and his greed. He will not stop until he strips your heirs of whatever he finds appealing.

How quickly the reaper cut short your youth, how dare the hag quell that smartness you displayed so gallantly, extinguish the fire that burned in your flesh, snuff out the warm breath, wilt that body that barely yesterday I depicted in its highest splendor. Suddenly your life ends, while fate leaves me, debilitated by infirmities, to suffer from this withered flesh, which was more likely to expire than yours. I cannot resign myself to the fact that so much beauty lies beneath the earth, which is now corrupting it. At least in some way—oh feeble consolation!—I succeeded in preserving it, in faithful and loving effigies. And these, beloved Duchess, are the images that endure in my memory. They will survive us.

Comedy of Apparitions

For Pablo Picasso

I.

In the center is the queen, her throne the back of her mount. She is nude. She dazzles with her robust thighs, stupifies with her fleshy spheres. (May your bosom suckle us, oh prodigious woman!) The matron holds sway. Her roly-poly cherub plays between the horse's hooves. The old man contemplates the glory of life—the desired one—with melancholy and serenity. His lady accompanies him, a beauty, mistress of his days and nights. She too is unclothed. Luscious, she rests a gentle hand on his shoulder. The old man wears a straw hat on his bald head. His sturdy body is both vigorous and senile. The outline of his figure wavers. The curves of the women are clean.

II.

Smaller than them all, from his corner he contemplates the scene. At times he enters it entirely, dressed the same way as the other characters. They pose. They are imposing. Erect, on a Roman chariot—embellished by ornate reliefs—the archer looks straight ahead, like his cat. The old man has the stature of a child; he presses his back against the belly and fleshy inner thighs of the vestal, to affirm the continuation of life, no doubt. The old child, with the face of a hairless monkey, observes the spectacle with ecstasy and amazement. His disguise suggests that he is participating in the fiesta, his expression that he is bidding farewell.

III.

On her dashing steed, on the rearing beast, on that genius of furious force, harnessed with trappings for the festival, goes the Amazon in her display of voluptuous power: portent of her body with the seven doors—whoever sees them feels the urge to cross their thresholds. Her round breasts bounce to the rhythm of the gallop. Velvety down cushions the soft entrance to the abode of delight. All passes between horse and rider. Majestic, both of them circle the track, while the trainer, in top hat and tails, commands the equestrian parade with cracks of his whip. A gentleman in breeches, jerkin, ruff collar, and curled wig awaits. He holds one dove in his hand; another is in flight. The old man, rugged, a midget king, is doddering. He has put on an embroidered jacket, cap, and formal slippers. He walks leaning on his stick, crude scepter, that knotty pole. Vain, with his showy suit of popinjay, he struts before the young girl, the most beautiful one he was able to imagine. Comical king of the deck, he plots a clown's trick to surprise his lady. With such carnivalesque comedy perhaps he can amuse her, perhaps seduce her, in his manner. No other recourse remains to him.

IV.

It is he, there is no doubt. The one now playing the role of protagonist chose to be this bald, short, muscular, pot-bellied Bacchus, so satisfied with his aspect. With his crown of vine leaves, he shows himself stark naked. Provocative, he pierces with his small, flashing eyes. Just so he exhibits himself, flamboyant, as if defying all prudence with his brio. And though he stands in contrast to the young gentlemen and ladies who celebrate him, harmony prevails, a tender peacefulness reigns. The smooth conforms with the rough, the hairless with the shaggy. The same happens with the *majas*: the clothed one corresponds to the nude. Certainly it is she, the inconstant, the same one who inflamed the deaf man, the other small and great, the formidable predecessor. This delicious lady never ceases to seduce. Our insatiable Bacchus has the nerve to take possession of the Duchess. No, he does not appropriate her, he borrows her. And, in his dream of omnipotence, enjoys her, both clothed and nude. Almost like his predecessor.

V.

Chunky, stocky, diminutive satyr, phallus ready for the assault, he looks content: he rubs his hands. His appetite always at the ready, free of guile, he is greedy. The Venus stretched out on the bed has opened her legs. The lips of her spreading vulva are an invitation to the feast, ready for the appetizing reception. Enveloping the swollen slit, cumuli of cushiony flesh, so much smooth softness to greet the muscular faun. Stunned, his eyes are rivetted on the ingress that is electrifying him. He knows that the amazing entry gives access to the fountain from which everything springs. He is no longer contemplating, all distance is abolished, already now, with nose, pencil, penis, he is penetrating her. Velázquez, master of simulcra, acquiescent, gracefully watches the game. In another of the comedies, he will be the actor and the old man will kibitz.

VI.

Now he is dressed as a harlequin. With the little finger of his left hand he holds the palette, with the others he grasps the bundle of brushes: those that await him. With the right hand he brandishes the one that delights in tinting those nacreous buttocks. Harlequin is absorbed in his enterprise: that of painter of goddesses. Convoked, once again, another of so many, the Venus of the Mirror, grandiose, brims over. Carnal chimera, incarnate in rosy volumes of illusion. The curvature of her belly bulges, her soft abundant bottom billows. Unctuous, sumptuous, the whole enthralls. Colossal in her divine concupiscence, she surely knows her influence: whoever looks at her is taken captive. The clown in his comedy of apparitions depicts the *pomona* who fulfills and enraptures him. Bonanza. He whitens her milky buttocks. With his oil he anoints her. The old man paints the Venus putting on make-up. The old man paints a painter painting a woman painting herself. The old man paints himself painting. That's how he lived. For him painting and living were inseparable, one same manner, both one and the same: prodigies.

The Blue Train Car

Construction for Noble Ladies

Kurt straightens and enlivens the ambience of his most noble ladies. He places circles of different sizes at distinct distances—astral order—suspended over a stormy firmament. Reddened rapture against celestial mechanics. He folds over the edge of the solar circle to avoid the tangency with the lilac. A liliaceaous moon flashes wanly in the ultramarine darkness. With a blackish line he blocks the rosy morning star. Then with two laths and a rod superimposed he constructs a central triangle. On each of the two vertices he installs a disc. A geometric organization orders the impulse. On the right goes the low candlestick, with its dark eye. Below he puts a lumpy circle; its chiaroscuro feigns the spherical. Above he introduces the great brass planisphere, with its sky-blue sea and reddish earth. It is traversed by a vertical brown lath. Then nearby he places wheels from a baby carriage, one whole and two broken. Their spokes make them insubstantial, reveal the background. The white rim of the tires stands out clearly. The impassive clockwork struggles with the flares of the warm colors. And in complete promiscuity with the strange, Kurt distributes the effigies of his ladies. They can hardly be seen, except for a semi-nude bust posed horizontally and in profile. Could it be Anna Blume, the favorite, with her long sensual neck? Kurt inserts and juxtaposes like with the most unlike. He seeks, makes, dares the most unusual juxtapositions. Because of its old grayish color with touches of red, the piece of wood shaped like a mushroom or an arrow looks like a rat. It abuts the rectangle of cream-colored paper, a clearly legible coatroom check. In spite of the pencil marks that smudge them, one can also read the newspaper clippings pasted on the left side. Straight white lines mark paths that connect whatever they encounter, a ruddy cloudiness submerges scattered shapes. The solid and the hazy engage in their battles and agree to their liaisons. Thus Kurt goes along composing the universe most fitting for his ladies.

The year is 1919. Captivated by the incessant diversity of the world, Kurt's art becomes more and more collect-art. In this particular construction he sets out to combine the greatest possible accumulation of heterogeneous materials, wishes to abolish the distinction between nobles and plebeians. In contrasted concordance, he makes the pictorial illusion coexist with the emplacement of material objects. Here as never before, the flat image cohabits with solid, prominent, salient masses.

His crowded collage is almost complete, yet not entirely. Kurt sees that something is missing but does not know what. He will not stop until he finds the object that will finish it. At the moment all his efforts come to nothing. The work puts up a resistance hard to overcome.

Daily Walk

With no fixed goal in mind, he wanders through the city, scrutinizing attentively in all directions. He looks like a bloodhound, nose almost always to the ground. Every so often he stops, bends over, picks something up, puts it in one of his pockets. Careful in his way of dressing, almost elegant, with dark suit and gleaming black shoes, Kurt makes his daily rounds. Just in case, he carries along his austere grip, which gives him a certain air of jurisconsult (of operetta) or, rather, of a traveling salesman. (His parents had kept a dress shop; they both suffered from bad teeth; that's how Kurt remembers them, with constant affection). This zealous vigilance, that dissimulated detective who passes for petit bourgeois detects what nobody else sees, he sees like nobody else. That lynx spots the tram ticket lying intact on the drab pavement. Attracted, drawn as if by a magnet to the rectangle of pale sky-blue, he picks it up and carries it away. Who if not Kurt would, with pristine glance, notice a used ticket? Beside it he finds a reddish capsule, faintly shining, a little farther on a matchbox with the blushing face of a smiling girl, a golden cigar ring, then a mother-of-pearl button. Close by, Kurt sights a row of trash cans with apparent parsimony (the impostor pretends a false disdain), but excited by the probable treasure, he comes near, furtively lifts each lid, and examines the contents with watchful eye. He works like a customs agent in search of contraband. When he glimpses something that might interest him, he pokes with precision, with meticulous tidiness, until he traps the coveted prey. He puts it in his grip (rip rip) and continues his traipsing (sing sing). Traverses (verses), stops (tops), slows (lows), turns (urns), coils (oils), letting himself be carried along by his hunter's instinct (by his stunts for tincture). He tracks traces that hint at bounteous finds. Goes to wherever he has inklings (clings clings nervously to his cigar) that his luck may be favorable (able? able?). He knows that the best and greatest part of his search depends on a happy alliance (fifty fifty) between perspicacity and chance. Kurt relies on chance ruling (how much and how) that adventure, that persistence that is life. He adores his fortuitous supplier (fortune) of surprising encounters, his knotter (his master) of unsuspected junctures. Now he leaves the avenues, walks into the maze (to be amazed) of the old quarter. He enters buildings, greets the cats of the neighborhood with affection, especially that striped lazybones, keeps going all the way to the inner courtyards. He sees balconies (they delight him) with geraniums, begonias, and carnations. While a yellow petal sways and falls, the kitty swipes his paw over his jet black muzzle. Kurt searches through the nooks where all the crusts, the cracked and discarded, come to rest. Among the castoffs he spies and traps anything that might be of use to him. He continues his rounds and in passing (search is not all) contemplates the facades, delights in the interplay of apertures and projections, the subtle interchanges of light and shadow, the luster and attenuation of the colors, with their tones, ranges, and contrasts. For Kurt, no matter where, beauty is lying in wait.

The Fisherman's Haul Tadah! Dada!

Now Kurt wanders through the industrial district. He knows the location of each factory like the palms of his hands. Metallurgy, confectionery, and paper plants are his favorites. The closer he gets, the more his eyes gleam. He rubs his hands: greed is goading him. He licks his lips in anticipation, feels like jumping. He goes in search of the appetizing piles of leftovers, the great feast that awaits him. Soon he glimpses promising heaps, assumes the fishing will be profitable, maybe even a miraculous spectacle (tackle, tackle, fisherman, the sea of filth, tackle). He crouches over the clippings. Picks up metal pieces of singular outline, scraps of cardboard and other materials of surprising shapes. Touches and enjoys (as he revels in touching the skin of Anna Blume, as he revels in Anna Blume with the twenty-seven senses she gratifies), enjoys the textures, consistencies, the sensory gratifications that each material offers him. He gathers tubes and rods, colored strips, remnants of printed material. Like a child who plays with whatever is within reach, everything tempts him. For him, each material possesses its own personality, complexion, nature, each displays its particular signs of identification. Kurt perceives even the most subtle. Lover of all materials, solely for pleasure, his unsurpassable skill knows how to combine all kinds in order to enhance them. So he collects some of everything, and whatever he finds he uses to advantage. His art could now do without brushes and tubes, become scarce and expensive. The world emerges barely, barely reappears, it reappears in shambles from that brutal war, the most destructive of all that can be remembered. Defeated and ravaged, Germany sacrificed so many of its best artists, the most rebellious, the most promising. After the disaster, like many people who manage to subsist in whatever way they can, Kurt makes do with what he finds at hand, with throwaways. With these he reconstructs the new face of the world.

Precious Trash

Now Kurt ventures through the city's outskirts, where garbage dumps abound, because this amiable gentleman, dressed so neatly, goes into ecstasy when turning over mountains of trash. That's where luck plays its most surprising games. Kurt knows overly well that the most unexpected things end up as leftovers. The city's inhabitants dump pieces of their lives. And discards usually have a patina of age, a quality that nothing or no one could bestow. Work utensils preserve the warmth of the hands that held them and used them, keep an echo of the human touch still throbbing in them. The weight emanating from these things moves Kurt, the soul of each implement makes him tremble. He senses the story pulsing in each scrap. For every object that he recuperates, he knows that he saves, awakens, a latent past. Kurt rescues a faded strip of passementerie, a frame with the plaster peeling, wooden laths and boards that time with its innate talent stripped of paint, pieces of crockery, a tin plate with a wintry landscape, a mask with the nose smashed, the body of a headless doll, a chip of pink ivory.

With his grip and pockets full, tired out by his explorations, Kurt hurries back to his house. He is anxious to display his booty, to delight in observing each article with the care it demands. He wishes to contemplate each item according to its own way of being.

The Jigsaw Puzzle

Kurt enters his comfortable, respectable house on Wildhausenstrasse, goes into his studio, and whatever remains outside is erased. He enters his kingdom of wonders. All hurry, burdens cease. Kurt is now supreme master of his belongings, lord of his actions. He empties his bulging pockets and with meticulous solemnity puts away his gray grocer or bookkeeper's overcoat. As usual he wears his bow tie and an icy white celluloid collar. His short, well-trimmed hair is parted carefully on the right. Tall and thin, he moves with a ridiculous stiffness. His circumspection calls to mind a mechanical doll. Self-satisfied, Kurt settles in his most personal spot, the zone of exception where he arbitrarily decides on arrangements, where his taste regulates every stratagem. But before examining the contents of his grip, he contemplates the large jigsaw puzzle that holds and preoccupies him. That bounteous picture offered in tribute to his beautiful ladies seems capable of admitting any addition.

But no. So close is the complicity between its components, so intimate the composition, that it rejects any new arrival. At the same time, the weights do not keep the required equilibrium. The collage limps; this can be felt simply by looking at it. Kurt knows that the more advanced this type of assemblage, based on contraries, on unusual agreements, the more difficult it becomes to add anything. He decides to review the loot of the day, to see if any one of the pieces can be accepted as a member of this highly sensitive crew.

The Treasure Chamber

Kurt paints and assembles in his own house. He has always lived there with his family. His father gave him two rooms on the ground floor; the larger one he converted into a studio. More than an artist's atelier it resembles a second-hand shop, the warehouse of a scrap dealer or of theatrical props. Filled with trinkets and thingamajigs, what purpose could such a large collection of useless objects possibly serve? But Kurt finds total contentment in this Ali Baba cave. A sort of attic where all unnecessary things land, here in his select, exclusive trash dump, Kurt is at his ease; when he is ensconced there he feels like a prince retired to his private cabinet of curios. In his bailiwick he puts together his outlandish artifacts, arrays fetishes, adorns fantastic puppets.

How can such an accumulation of junk bring him so much joy? For Kurt, objects possess a mysterious presence, their silence preserves something secret, strangely intrinsic: it veils and unveils. Impenetrable, unpredictable, they agree or disagree with their users. At times they captivate, at times intimidate. Kurt feels that they gaze at him from the other side, with disturbing peculiarity. He finds the upsetting presence of things a cause for wonder. Even the most useless baubles fascinate him. Kurt is dumbfounded by leavings. Mounds of daily trash: airhole that sucks him in, magnet that attracts him, snare that ensnares him. Just as the suspicion of a hidden vestige lures the archeologist, trash arouses Kurt, obsesses him, compels him to excavate without pause. That is Kurt: the first archeologist of the modern city. What the city spews out, continually scatters and piles up, that surplus litter with which the city relieves and expresses itself, constitutes for Kurt a deposit of inexhaustible beauty.

Kurt Explains His Purpose

I record the traces of my transit. I mark my personal time and the convulsion of the era that immerses me and that I traverse. It is my wish that everything I collect may transcribe its existence, show how its life persists coincidental with mine. Thus we fuse together what I see, what I use with feeling. Thus we merge. Chosen and arranged by me, these things that I rescue from abandonment come to share in my selfhood. They are in themselves and they extend me. We are joined. They carry me in them. They go with themselves and with me. Put in their place, the site and arrangement they demand, they assume a look that I make conform. Concomitantly, I seek a common accord, a discordant accord for them. I assemble the inexhaustible reality constantly offered to me. I use what comes to my hands, what shows its face, what chance puts within my reach. Thus just as I perceive the multiplicity of what occurs at each moment, I accommodate and adjust scattered pieces of the world. I accept, celebrate its irreducible variation. I do not seek unity, only a possible, transitory concert. I intone the chant and disenchantment of the world.

Everything turns into MERZ: fragmentation, dispersal, mixture, vertigo. My world is MERZ; I am MERZ; merzer, everything I wish, live, make, I merzify. That's why I employ any material, from flimsy paper to heaviest metal. Just as opposites coexist in my surroundings, I put them side by side in my assemblages, even though they repel and loathe each other. To bind them I intersect them with furious bands. Against the impassive architecture I set my impetuous brush strokes. I orchestrate the battle of straight lines and curves with what is dictated by my instincts. Also, in each one of us, the uniform city with its parallelepipeds, its orderly traffic patterns, cohabits with intricate labyrinths, thick tangles. In the same way, my art interweaves contemporaneous and counterposed worlds. Pitiful shreds, pieces separated by mutilation, here ousted objects concur; in reconciling they find comfort: beautify.

Redeemer of Castaways

Kurt perpetuates the worthless, whatever increasing consumption condemns to disappear. Voracious and diarrhea-ridden colossus, the city swallows and eliminates all goods, all substance. Barely employed, things immediately fall into disuse. The minute they become valuable, they quickly depreciate. And what is most moving to Kurt is this destitution. Where the utilitarian ends, Kurt begins to operate. Where the economy belittles, Kurt values. Explorer of wastelands, oh redeemer of castaways, persevere in your search, pursue what nobody would perceive without you. No one reveals as you do how significant the insignificant can be. Nobody captures as you do the innermost appeal of each scrap. You detect the rubble's powerful charge. That's why you call it poison. In measured doses, you say, it is compatible and stimulates; in excessive amounts it nauseates and kills.

    Kurt turns again to the construction of the picture in which he has carried agglomeration to extremes. This hodgepodge—he reflects—makes a world, figures my sphere. It is like the machine of the universe. Never was the consistency of applied objects greater in my work. Those masses conform to the whole, but at the same time keep their clear, compact, unavoidable difference. Kurt amuses himself organizing this feast of beggars, delights in reconciling this troupe of outcasts, this formidable fox-trot of folderol.

How To Remedy the Shortcoming

In spite of the profusion, the construction teeters. It needs a counterweight. Below, on the right side, an area remains inert. The components are not compatible. Their passivity depresses them. They require something that will arouse them, make them cohere. Kurt searches in his storeroom for whatever might remedy the shortcoming. He tries a piece of grainy wood. Stirs in the button box: a thousand eyes stare at him. He thinks a big one, dark crimson, can supply what is missing. He chooses a few, places them on the ladies, none satisfy him. None enchants, none works the miracle. He tries out springs, spools, cog wheels. Nothing fits. He falls back on the cupboard of papers, his collection of postcards (his mania), colored prints, tokens, clippings, letters received, tickets with cancellation stamps, labels, his expired ration coupons. Every piece of paper that passes through his hands ends up in this cupboard. The world is turning into an immense paper store. A paper certifies every act, every status. A paper for each passage. A paper to identify, a paper to authorize, to pay and be paid, to receive and to cancel. Entrance paper, exit paper. Signs and countersigns of paper. Whirlwind of papers, the papers waltz, carried along by the cyclone until they cover the sky. Kurt knows the quality and function of each paper, what it is and what it represents. How much life, how much anxiety, how much sorrow there is in each paper. But it is not paper that his picture needs. It demands something corporeal, bulky. He goes to the corner of odds and ends, of single pieces. Turns over and over. Here again he finds nothing suitable. It would be better—so he deludes himself—to provoke a surprising contrast, put in something brand-new. Kurt also has a store of trinkets. He prizes his collection of tacky junk: bargain-basement ceramic pieces, little statues of cloying colors, vases of grating taste, geegaws so ugly they become almost beautiful. With great care, Kurt reviews his eyesores. That porcelain shepherdess with her staff and her beribboned lamb, her sky-blue and red organza dress might be just what is needed. He puts her in the inanimate spot. Vertical, horizontal, leaning, upside down, he proves that in no way does she hit if off. Wherever placed, she is repudiated. Nothing goes, nothing gets along, nothing agrees. All persistence is in vain. To make up for the disappointment, the panacea without any doubt is Anna Blume.

Kurt Invokes the Charm of Anna Blume

Rather than tempting luck with objects, dealing with those dour demons and getting daubed by brushes, it would be better to play with words, with their beautiful sounds, their timbres, as if they were colors. Preferable to savor them there where they are formed and resound, in the mouth that pronounces them, slice them into bites, revert them, mash them at will, eviscerate them with glee, ratatatata tataratata tatarará, smash them, turn over the pieces, fákete bee bee zee, then put them together as you please (embellish embrangle the tangle embroider embroil and emblazen embellembrangembroidembroiemblazen). Nothing more heartwarming than to render the daily homage to the enchantment of Anna Blume: please her. She, his favorite, his beloved, comes and goes through his head, her going startling, her returning marvelous. Thou my mine I thy thine with me in me with thee in thee—Kurt invokes her so that she may pull him from the mire. In evoking her, everything wished for comes to pass, to everything she accedes and everything good succeeds. Everything circles and conveys. Wondrously she consents. A thousand eyes look and see, a thousand doors open on the gifts of Anna Blossom. She, the most attractive girl that can be imagined, captivates Kurt, consoles, confers, and guides him: inspires him. To her he dedicates his umpteenth poem. The words flow, leap, roll, veer, revolve. Under the influence of the splendid redhead, the vowels vocalize, the consonants concertize, in high spirits the dentals diddle, the sibilants hiss, the implosives explode; not only the syllables, but the colons and commas get all worked up, all the signs celebrate the glory of Anna Blume. Because of her charm, the birds redden, the roses cerulean, and the gazelles green. Praise to Anna, talisman, bride whose name drips gently like a candle. Carol, call, corolla, she Anna Blume gladdens, ANNA, A——N——N——A—— colors life in fabulous fashion, sweetens it, showers it with wonders.

Farce with Ruler and Compass

In the white room with the tall windows the drafting boards are in a row. At the third from the left Kurt is drawing with a ruler and compass. With his green eyeshade and his cellophane cuffs like a croupier, he draws plans of metallic machines. No one seeing him so concentrated on his work would suspect that inside he is thinking nonsense: spinning fancies. He is dreaming of a column full of convolutions, nooks and crannies where he can store all the things he adores. Here every person he loves will have their own compartment with one of their belongings, whatever represents them best. For Theo, a piece of his sky-blue tie; for Hans, a lock of his porcupine hair; for Nelly, a kiss, the impression of her scarlet lips, and cuttings from her redred nails; for himself he would add various examples of his existence, not just photographs, vestiges, fetishes, also an ampoule of his blood and a flask of his urine. He would even install his guinea pig in a comfortable cave, construct a run for it like a city burrowed into the mountain. No one seeing him handle the ruler with surgical precision could suppose that this serious draftsman, while tracing his rigorously straight lines over the graph paper, is composing ditties, tongue twisters, palindromes, chitter-chatter, that in his head carols a grim glim gnim bimbim, chimes the bum bimbim bam or the bem bem, that his tui tui tui and his te te te chirp only for him. No one seeing his composure, his skillful gestures, that look absorbed in the cross section of a connecting rod, would suspect that Kurt is on a spree, amusing himself by imagining himself walking along the white walls and the ceiling with his soles inked for printing, as often he leaves the trace of his wanderings with his rubber stamps. Every three steps he gives a leap and a shout. Now he embraces the flirtatious secretaries, intertwines with them and whirls them in a dizzying polka and a frenetic Cossack number. Every so often he stops, blows rainbow colored bubbles from his mouth and from his ass, lets out farts phenomenal but not fetid, his windiness smells of lavender. Everyone who passes by the plant is wearing a disguise; Kurt keeps designing his own with one part from each outfit; his disguise changes constantly.

Mechanical Skill

Truthfully, it doesn't bother you, Kurt, to draw plans of machines, devote yourself to an exercise that curbs your turbulence. Although you cram your pictures with figures, the heap is organized over a framework of circles and rectangles that provide a geometrical support. You always treat space like a geometer. That's why drafting appeals to you. You have become an expert in graphic design and you go into ecstasies over machines. You are fascinated by the meshing of gears, the mechanical transmission of movement makes you marvel. You admire locomotives with their powerful steaming pistons; those giants becoming more and more aerodynamic, faster and faster, dazzle you. Automobiles astound you, airplanes leave you open-mouthed. You follow with close attention the rapid progress of so many devices that endlessly multiply the capacity of production, of transformation and transportation of man. Everything inevitably becomes mechanized. Soon, you think, even painting by hand will turn out to be antiquated. Art is also obliged to enter the mechanical kingdom. The artist will cease to be an artisan who fabricates one-of-a-kind objects. Works will be reproduced in thousands of copies, like the postcards that you enjoy printing. Everyone will be able to own works of art. The artist will be the intermediary between the mechanical world and the human, will reconcile men with artifacts, humanize machines. You don't sense, you cannot yet know, that the machine will subjugate man once again, increase endlessly his power of destruction and regulate his existence, at every point impose on him the same harsh hand. The industrial order will expand its empire to overwhelm man and lead him toward another total war. You don't know, Kurt, you cannot envision the coming of the foul-mouthed outrageous vociferator, the mustachioed Lucifer with his cohort of thugs. You don't yet glimpse the hegira of people in uniform, letting themselves be led by a ferocious leader to a new extermination. You still don't foresee the arrogance and the assault of the imperious rulers of the warring regime. You don't see its multitudinous idolaters marching, arms extended, in unison proclaiming German strength with the sound of their jackboots. You don't suspect that the painter of yesteryear risen to despot will clamp over art too a Caesarean order. You don't suspect that your work will be reviled by him, thrown on the pyres of the next inquisition.

Cutter-Composer

His day's work in the metallurgy plant finished, Kurt, with his habitual neatness, again puts on his hat, takes his cane, and goes out once more. At this hour the streets are jammed with people. A short distance from the factory, he happily joins the stream of strollers. So discreet is the correctness of his petit bourgeois clothes, so correct his discretion, so harmonious the dimension, so composed the accommodation, that it becomes noticeable, turns out to be ridiculous. Here he comes with his gait both distinguished and farcical. He comes with his fitted mole-gray suit and plaid vest, stiff wing collar and tie in the exact center of the shirt front. He throws his hair back, uncovering his forehead, but a few wayward locks come forward or make whirls. He flaunts a respectable, Germanic little moustache. He looks like a gentleman, but his jacket pulls at the waist, making a few ugly wrinkles in the back. With his usual good nature, Kurt smiles sweetly, passes among the people as if asking pardon with a stiff bow; he behaves with a somewhat affected amiability, and often excuses himself. Polite, but rash, he manages to please but then becomes a nuisance.

Certainly, although he may be called a painter, Kurt looks like what he actually is for part of the day: a technical draftsman. He draws with precision any piece of machinery, but he handles brushes clumsily. No matter, he never stops trying. He plashes and paints and paints to become a better painter. Rather than tubes, which he has replaced by cans of ordinary paint, he enjoys playthings to be assembled. Because he loves typography, he collects rubber stamps. He has them made with drawings and inscriptions that can be repeated and combined. Perhaps he would have liked working in the post office, keeping busy franking letters, pasting and sealing, pasting and sealing. As he did as a child in his school notebook, every time he sees something printed, what an itch, he gets the urge to cut it out and paste it somewhere. And in that game of clipping and pasting he finds tremendous pleasure. Instead of a painter, Kurt is a cutter-composer.

The Powerful Disparity

After the war, that colossal hecatomb, the world is transformed at a quickening pace. Everywhere razing and constructing. Everything is modernized, aligned and smoothed, squared and polished. That's why Kurt wanders in search of what remains, what is left aside, what is damaged. Kurt looks for the tattered things that leveling discards. In the midst of the brand-new, a common something stays, resists, is different, keeps its discrete particularity. A way of fading, of wearing, a dent, a stripe, those cracks distinguish, temporalize, manifest a mode of existing: humanize. Beneath uniformity Kurt perceives a force as powerful as smoothing out, if not more so; something that strives to circumvent the even, to split the unified. Kurt pursues the dissimilarity, cultivates that irrepressible dissent that endlessly generates a variety of objects. Kurt assembles the divergent, takes advantage of the powerful disparity of things. And to depict what he undergoes, the great jumble that submerges and drives everything, he puts together what he finds, what capricious fortune provides him, the trivial, the discordant. He organizes the conglomeration and the mixture, suspends them in a precarious equilibrium, at a wavery point where what is grouped together at the same time disperses.

Wandering and Dithyramb

Like an explorer venturing into strange territory, Kurt undertakes another expedition through the city. Another time he tries his luck: he walks at random. He searches for the remains of a recent past, soon to disappear, looks to the right and to the left, prying. Every so often he picks something up and keeps it. Joyful stroller, he rejoices in the street spectacle, in whatever happens around him. On the alert, he takes note of the varied and incessant movement of the city, the changing landscape, the swift passing of the cars, the diverse humanity on the move, the decorated show windows where hieratic mannequins suggest the latest garments—outer and inner—listens to the sonorous magma that melds voices, motors, and peals of bells. In the midst of the bustle, he sees a little white dog with a black spot over its right eye. He trots like a metronome, with short quick steps, his tail straight but keeping perfect time. Every now and then, like Kurt, he stops. Examines something, sniffs it; if it suits him, he eats it; if not, he leaves it and continues his plundering. Kurts feels much sympathy for that vagabond dog; he supposes that he too lets himself be led along by his fancy, that he too doesn't know where he's going.

So that his stroll will be even more pleasurable, Kurt decides to make a stop at the café with the stained-glass windows. He sits at a table next to the biggest window; from there he has a wide view of the street. He orders a glass of amber beer. Notes how it foams. Takes a look at the clientele, above all at the women at the next table, as distinguished as those of his picture, he imagines. He sees their hats with velvet flowers and with tulle veiling part of their features, their powdered faces with red circles on their cheeks, the oval carmine of their appetizing lips, their hands bared or gloved, the harmonious folds of their dresses, their prominent bosoms, the line of their silk stockings, the curve of their insteps, their graceful and pointed shoes. He compares all of them to his precious Anna Blume; not one, not even the most beautiful, can measure up to this paragon. He takes his notebook from his pocket and prepares a rosary of verses in praise of her, the prodigious one who showers miracles wherever she passes. Whoever sees Anna when she appears knows that happiness exists. As she passes, lilies spring up, roses scatter, grapes ooze, and flocks of doves cuddle. When Anna smiles, the world bears fruit; when she laughs, apples blush. It is enough that she show herself for the sky to clear and sprout rainbows. Anna blues, greens, purples, yellows, oranges, violets. As she tints, she contents; as she perfumes, she transports. The aroma that emanates from Anna intoxicates the orange blossoms. Mastiffs are anxious to lick her. No shadow resists her radiance. Before her beauty the suicidal do not take their lives, they desist, regain hope. When Anna comes near, stones feel an effluvia of joy penetrate and lighten them, clocks speed up their ticktock, crocodiles hiccup their hallelujahs, trees play tarantellas with their wooden fingers, statues become merry and flirt with her, the crowded avenues expand, adorn themselves, and begin meandering; to acclaim her, factories makes their sirens wail and their chimneys whistle, airplanes peck and pirouette in her honor. Anna imbues the world with her beauty and the world emulates her, becomes annafied.

The Blue Train Car

Relaxed by the pause and enchanted by the memory of Anna Blume, annafilled, Kurt resumes his walk. Although few notice him, he leaves his table in the café smiling to the right and to the left to show how much he relishes that moment of his life. He continues his walk, his nosing about, through the center. As usual, his pockets are crammed full. The magnet of chance directs him toward the park. He admires some chestnut trees, the solid strength of the trunks and the well-proportioned shape of the crowns. He appreciates the graceful foliage of the larches, a celadon green so light they seem almost suspended. Kurt would like to give to his sculptures some of that same vivid harmony. He reflects on the art demanded by an impetuous, reckless, restless time. Art needs to be invigorated, vitalized, recover all its primitive force. That's what Kurt was thinking while still casting furtive glances at the trash cans. Little boys circle in flocks riding their tricycles, cars, and scooters. Others shout, run, throw multicolored balls. Lovely nursemaids shashay past, rolling babies in their carriages. How enchanting is that delicate little girl wearing a sailor suit and rolling her hoop. In the midst of the children's clamor, a bellow, a roar, and a shriek reverberate through the park. Through the branches appear the gates of the zoo. Kurt starts toward the nearby meadow. Scattered couples frolic on the grass, near the parasols sparkling in the sun. Kurt would also like to let himself fall on the tender grass, even though he is so dressed up. He searches for a solitary spot and no sooner does he enter the meadow than a curious object attracts his attention. He picks it up and sees it is part of a toy. It is half of a blue train car made out of tin. Its doors and windows are outlined in red. He suddenly feels certain that this find will allow him to finish the construction for noble ladies. He immediately begins his trek home. The minute he arrives he rushes to the easel where the picture is waiting. He puts the train car below, on the right, in the inanimate part, in the shadowy area. He places it over the hair of the lady, almost vertically, as if it were rushing headlong into the void. The train car blends and the area revives. Relieved, Kurt savors this fortuitous victory. For the moment everything seems to be in order. He must let the picture rest. He presumes that he can call it finished. Tomorrow, when he is detached and has some distance from his creature/creation, he will know for certain.

Jocular Interlude: Kurt's Guffaws

Late at night, Kurts looks for distraction. He would like to forget his construction for a while. The best remedy against worries and setbacks, he well knows, is a visit with Charlie. He goes to the movies, to enjoy the new series of Chaplin's mime-dramas. This ragged dandy has the gift of lifting his spirits. In his pantomimes, his burlesque ballets, synchronized with the precision of a robot, Kurt finds a number of affinities with MERZ. At the moment the imaginative clown and the humorous painter have the same haircut, similar moustaches, resemblances that amuse Kurt very much. Kurt admires Chaplin's inventive buffoonery, the comical grace that allows him to come out of any predicament on top. But most of all, he appreciates the disjointed rhythm, constantly broken and recomposed, the variable and contrasting nature of the montage, its unforeseeable outcome. When Charlie waltzes around the ring boxing or does his farcical ice skating like an elf, with breathtaking skill, creating havoc with his cane, Kurt marvels at the hilarious choreography, with what aptness, what vertiginous cadence Charlie regulates his comedy of entanglements, how he stages his unsurpassable tricks, this spectacular acrobat. Chaplin also takes advantage of the most common objects, animates and dignifies rejects, retrieves and puts his personal stamp on leftovers. He uses gadgets in his own fashion, changes the common usage, appropriates in his own way any utensil, removes it from its function, changes the order of the world, recreates it according to his own measure, adapts it to return it in harmony with his own humanity, momentarily more inviting.

Soothed by Chaplin, Kurt then goes to the bar that artists frequent. He joins a group of his friends, boisterous and fervent advocates of everything new. With them he conspires against the pastists, contrives ridiculous categorical manifests, exaggerating the jumble, invents laughable recipes to fabricate absolutely modern works. Plans parties with fantastic high jinks, entirely unfettered spectacles where irreverence inverts everything and diverts everyone. His friends cheer him on, offer to help. Each participant contributes to this festive commotion. In this contest of craziness, witty ideas abound: outlandish clothes, hats with mad inscriptions, absurd shouted proclamations, music hall poses and skits, cacophonic poems, idiotic choruses, tableaux vivants, lampoons of cabaret numbers, like those at the Voltaire. Their imagination, which cuts any mooring, joyfully takes wing, urges them on: the crescendo of proposals become more and more radical, more grotesque, so ridiculous they are near sublime. They crack jokes and think of their side-splitting effects. Kurt's guffaws explode with irresistible joy, like broadsides. His salvos of jubilant energy echo throughout the room. The other people, startled, are also cheered, turn to look at the boy who wholeheartedly erupts, expending all his strength and desires in laughter; in friendly fashion, they smile at him and egg him on.

On the way home from the spree, Kurt's thoughts again turn to his ladies. Back in his house, he cannot resist the call of his construction, which suddenly beckons him late at night. He switches on the lamp in the studio, places his picture in full light. With renewed attention, he analyzes it meticulously. Luckily the train car is right at home, declaiming like a sultan in his finest chamber. But the assembly, perverse thing, still limps on the right. Before going to bed with Helmchen, almost as beautiful as Anna, he checks to see if his little boy Lehmann is sleeping peacefully and is well covered. Stretched out in the bed in the dark, while caressing Helma's smooth soft thigh, Kurt goes over his construction inch by inch, that variety show that's missing an actor, that trash sky missing a star of unknown magnitude.

The World is MERZ

The next morning, while tracing lines with a ruler in the drafting room of the metallurgy plant, Kurt has an inspiration. He suddenly knows that to complete the picture he needs the other half of the train car. He needs to find it but is obliged to wait until his workday as technical draftsman is over. The minute he gets out of the factory, he hurries to the place of the find. It grows late, the light dims. When he reaches the meadow, instead of entering it, he presumes it is better to go in the opposite direction. He heads straight toward the museums, on the way to the city park. Throughout the walk his glance sweeps the ground. When he reaches the edge of the park, the first thing he sees is the other half of the blue train car. Intact it lies on the grass. Nobody picked it up, nobody stepped on it. Half hidden, it had stayed waiting for Kurt. Excited, he picks it up and runs to his house. Quickly, prey in hand, he arrives and bends over the construction. He places that half on the same side as the other but above. He puts it over the wooden triangle, moves it around searching for the exact position, decides to install it between the yellow brass circle and the piece of red wheel. One of the spokes holds it. Here, as if leaning over the great orange circle, like a train that encircles the incandescent planet, it remains forever fixed. Through the little windows of the car can be seen the fiery colors of the background, the red-tinted clouds of the sunset.

The operation accomplished, he steps back a few paces to make sure that his picture now has exactly what it was missing, neither too much nor too little. At last the conclusion seems obvious, imposed both by palpable and visible evidence. The tensions and distensions, the heavy and the light, the attractions and rejections, the lively and the serene, cohere, everything connects, is reciprocally compensated, hallelujah, everything constellates. The disparity merzunites, unanimously vibrates to the rhythm of the merzonance. Here the world becomes MERZ, merzarise, merzarouse: merzerupt.

Spectacles

Pastime

Immense and smooth rondure: its brightness is blinding. The room is surrounded by doors. Each person steps through his own. They land here, like me. They rush in headlong. The clarity is a surprise. They stop, look around, stroll about. Nobody knows anybody.

We walk around separately, come together, disband. I see a girl with a friendly face, she looks like me: disoriented, unprotected. We look at each other, she smiles at me. I go toward her, we need each other. Someone has come—I notice—through all the doors, except for one. On that one we concentrate our attention. Music, more and more sustained, fills the entire space. It reverberates through the glittering cupola, penetrates, ululates. We begin to sway, lift our arms and swing them to the beat. The rhythm cuts, we clap hands; stamp, stamp, we march vigorously, marking the step. The music shifts, switches. It becomes frenetic. We whirl around ardently, with contortions more and more violent. Later it grows quiet, becomes melodic, murmurous, we glide smoothly, lightly, until it ceases. Someone points at a spot. All outstretched index fingers converge there. But nothing and nobody is there. The fingers circle the large space: they pursue a prey that refuses to perch. Finally they become fixed: indicate the door through which no one has entered. Through it comes the master of ceremonies.

In full regalia he wears a tuxedo with satin lapels. He takes off his top hat and gives a gallant greeting. The company gathers round him. The murmuring ceases. In a well-modulated voice, with courteous gestures and snowy smile, he proposes a game. Each player will choose a letter. The letters can be repeated but only up to a certain number. No letter of the alphabet is excluded. I assume that door used by the emcee connects with other rooms. I ask myself what fortune goes with each letter. I suspect that one will permit the player to keep advancing.

"Choose the letter you like best," shouts the emcee as if he were advertising something. "Don't hesitate, ask me for one."

I, like so many others, vacillate. I don't know what the game hides, I don't know the intention of the organizer. I consult with my friend. We examine all the possibilities. We decide in favor of the symbolic numbers; she chooses the seventh letter, I the thirteenth. To get the game going, the emcee turns to the gambit of color:

"A black, E white, I red, U green, O blue," he chants in a singsong, certain of his seduction.

Various people opt for the vowels. The emcee takes them from his top hat and hands them out. But there are not as many vowels as requests. Those dissatisfied veer toward the consonants. B, L, R, S soon find their bettors. Not so—naturally—for K, Ñ, Q, W. The most malicious hang back, distrust, guess that they have to choose the leftovers. The ghostly H or the Y, that hybrid. The emcee keeps insisting on the correspondences: "C gray, D lilac, F cobalt, N coral, P carmine, T maroon, Z turquoise," he insinuates to tempt the remiss.

All the letters end up being taken. When the alphabet is exhausted and each participant has his own letter, the emcee says the game is over. Anxiously, we await the results. Expectation increases. The emcee has put on his top hat. He says nothing. The tension of the players keeps rising. Imperturbable, the emcee declares that there is no winner and no loser. Great consternation. Then a torrent of protests.

"It may be," he cautions, "that to each letter belongs a certain fortune, favorable for some, fateful for others. Each one will find out for himself. I know nothing about chance. I have done my part. My role consists simply in entertaining the crowd so that they forget the wait, temporarily, so that they won't despair."

That said, the master of ceremonies bows and then leaves us. He goes out the door he came in. Who knows whether he will return.

Crossing

We caught sight of the peak from the brambles. The sky was clouded over and icy gusts of wind were stirring up the ashes. We ate roots and chewed leaves without swallowing them, until we felt somewhat satisfied. Then we wrapped our feet again and started walking toward the brilliance. There was a sound like surf. The dryness became more intense. There were neither paths nor footprints to be seen; only salt, refluxes. Then Kid Rogers appeared. He said his lines with so much feeling that the audience, very moved, applauded him. And we had to wait motionless until he had finished before we could go on.

Why Bother to Read It

From the very first words, anyone caught up by his work has a foreboding for what comes next, knows the moment when the gradient of the poem will carry him inevitably to these colors—pale blue, violet, sulphur, lung rose, ash, milky white—or to certain objects—sheets, fingernails, flasks, oceans, erasers, eyelids, walls, brooms, mirrors, bees, bodies—thunderous guffaws, that there will be sandstorms, incessant drips, cracks and freezes, and that finally everything will be one big hodgepodge or there will go floating off into emptiness heads of hair, horned heads, bulging eyes, papers, rags, bills. In the universe, in this viscous jumble of fragmented bits, nothing will be what it was and nothing will be recognizable. I know: from the beginning I have known where I am being dragged.

Happiness

Tempted by the heap, I go in, searching for the object that will give me what I am lacking. This hole is a lot like a garbage dump. I enter the kingdom of castoffs. Pass by domestic appliances. Scan, touch. Premature fossils parade by: toasters that electrocute, ramshackle stoves, radios from the lower Quatenary, Paleozoic television sets, Bronze Age record players. Then come the piles of unmatched dishes: cracked plates, cups without handles, severed platters, crusty casseroles. Stragglers that stubbornly hang on, reprobates, these penitents ask forgiveness. (No, no, they are not purged, they already fill, jam-pack Avernus). Last straw of desolation, they give me the shivers: leprous mirrors, mutilated furniture, briefcases of dried-up skin, fecal-colored valises. Farther along, old clothes hang in a row: vestiges of used-up lives, the poor old life that goes to join the sea. Too much service of the dead. I flee toward an accumulation of junk. From a box I take out a pillowcase with the initials J.H. embroidered on a violet-colored background; take out a faint still life (on the back there's an inscription and a date); take out a tangle of spools of thread, yellowed lace, some buttons and a pencil stub. On the side I find two portraits of the same size: a couple looking straight ahead, their faces enhanced by touches of ingenuous color. They're not bad, the couple, countenances grave and features cheerful, because of the heightened color. I turn things over, rummage around in the darkness, inspect. Something shines: I exhume from the back of a shelf a slender vase (dazzling) of a rare iridescent blue, with a design of flowers in relief and ribs of intertwined arabesques. It radiates, I feel its aura, it possesses me. Saves me. I ransom this good fortune (oh, if it will only last) for very little money.

Spectacle

As usual, the Galíndez entertain me splendidly. We have supper in their suite off the corridor, on the upper gallery, where the boxes are. There they have their dining room. The dishes are abundant, highly seasoned: chicken in mayonnaise, suckling pig, ravioli, broiled lamb shanks, interminable feast. After a bit I am full. I ought to eat everything so as not to offend. To make matters worse, they are such chatterboxes and they keep serving me heavy red wine that goes right to my head. I smile like a booby, pretend to listen carefully. I fasten my eyes on the speaker; meanwhile I run my fingers over the carved moldings of the table, and look out of the corner of my eye at the table legs that end in lion's claws, or at the walls full of photographs and those strange paintings by Don Sinforoso. The head of a bald-headed doll above a lunar plain. They always tell me the same thing, it doesn't matter if you lose the thread of the conversation. Linda as an odalisque with a tambourine in her hand. Valerio as a scheming Venetian. A patio paved like a chessboard, a balustrade against a cloudless sky. Linda and Valerio wearing Greek peplums. I say yes to everything, I am having trouble keeping my head upright. Valerio as a Musketeer greeting the king. Now I am floating, although I am so overstuffed, such a dead weight, that only in dreams could I fly. Linda as a gypsy girl with a rose in her wig. A mirror, a glove, a starfish over a stony field. You know Valerio was so good in his role as the Sultan that Doña Matilde couldn't keep from crying in the scene where he pardons the abductor, although she has seen it so many times; and Linda got so much applause when she danced the fire dance; last night there weren't many people because the Santatonín family was celebrating the wedding of their daughter, they are so pretentious they asked for the downstairs hall for the banquet, but they were only allowed the room where the orchestra rehearses; even so, the noise could be heard on the stage, and the conductor of the orchestra complained and the director too, because the members of the chorus weren't in their places and those who had finished their act went down to the tacky wedding celebration to have a drink or to dance a few numbers. They not only had a piano, but also various musicians who were free that night. The noise was incessant, and when some of the spectators who had come to see the show heard about the wedding party, they got up and left, looking for diversion; some at least were polite enough to get a friend to take their place, so the hall wouldn't seem so empty. To be frank, Valerio didn't perform his role as gladiator as well as he did in the first performances, and the quality of the show has diminished because of the changes introduced by the director. People no longer want to leave their houses to watch such a long work, so tiring, although there are some really moving scenes: the one at the fair with the trained bear—it's Philip, the son of the Pietranellis—the jugglers, the ones who do the somersaults and later the dance of the stars of the night sky; the sets are quite good, but people look at them once when the curtain goes up and then forget about them, unless there are a lot of changes in the lighting. This is what the Galíndez say. While we were drinking and eating, eating and drinking, I was looking at the murky television screen; the damnable custom of eating with the TV on, the attention scattered among the supper, the guests, the TV screen. And to cap it all, just at that moment they were showing one of those complicated operas with crisscrossed love affairs, persecutions, duels, a dream in which everybody is turned into frogs and the high priest shuts them all up in an enchanted cave, and there they are set upon by infernal spirits, and there are great bangs on metal sheets for the thunder and a rain of cotton balls for the snow. The Galíndez had the TV on so they could see when their kids were about to appear. Valerio was going to play a sinister oak tree and Linda a lady of the night. Before going on stage they both came to warn us that it would be soon, in case we got distracted in conversation. The Galíndez told me they were getting lazier and lazier about attending the performances, that it wasn't like it used to be, that they only came to see Valerio or Linda; thank goodness Lalo and Tito wanted to have nothing to do with acting (Don Sinforoso says that in his day everybody was obliged to do some acting), the young ones want to be stagehands, or electricians, or ushers, and as far as Clothilde is concerned nobody can get her out of the dressing room or the beauty shop. Then we got up in a great hurry and all arranged ourselves in the boxes. We would have coffee when we returned during the first intermission. Naturally, I told them Valerio was masterly, that I recognized him, the third from the left, in spite of the fact that one couldn't see his face, muffled as it was with bark-colored cloth like the rest of his body, he really was scary in the semi-darkness moving in that stiff way just like a sinister oak tree. I recognized Linda too among the ladies of the night, all of them decked out in vaporous dresses with hoop skirts made of four white petals; so I went along with the Galíndez, poor things, always so attentive. The high priest disappeared in the midst of flames, the curtain closed, and all the lights were turned on; the chandelier in the center lit up and the chariot of muses and cherubim appeared on the ceiling. Exchanges of greetings, waves, and nods began among the spectators; quite circumspect, feigned. All the men had worn jackets and ties; the women kept an eye out for novelties, which they always found: new outfits, new hairdos, different make-up. The actors were forbidden to visit in the audience. We went back to the Galíndez' room to have coffee; we talked and talked, or rather they talked at me until very late. I wasn't worried, this week I was a spectator and could give myself the luxury of staying up all night. When I left, the theater was completely dark. I had a hard time finding my quarters.

Inside Your Caverns

...loaded down with dreadful visions, with rancorous visitants, irrepressible, the stampede erupts inside your contrite brain, ball of lava, anguish expands its imperious empire, besieges you and devastates you, pitiless, cuts you down, wipes out all bonanzas, all luck revokes and with its shadowy retinue, sovereign-like, implants itself, penetrates your caverns, whelms the boiling cauldron, kindles the fires of fear, buries you in them, wretched, looses over you the devouring cohorts and whatever wounds, whatever lacerates, suddenly, hidden tumult, your turbulent turbidity drowns you, your wits turn into a crab-infested quagmire, your mind is millstone, mortifying mortar, dying, opens up penitent and your wreckage files by, your infernal carnival, your parade of scarecrows that choke the life out of you, embitter your flesh, sting you, covered with slime you linger in this hour of rales, never ending, last gasp black and searing...

A morning sunbeam penetrates the blind, pierces the heart of your vampire.

So long, monsters, see you tomorrow.

Spaces

Cloistered in a room without windows.
Suddenly, blindingly, it is illuminated.
And it is death.

An enclosed space. As one traverses it,
it stretches, while remaining enclave.

Another, completely open. And one walks over
a surface that cannot be seen.

Of another, one knows it is spherical, but does not
know its center, nor the extension of its diameter.

Another is a cube without gravity:
any surface can be floor, wall, or ceiling.

In another, exclusively horizontal,
nothing, no one has any thickness.

Another where everything is inside.

Another where everything is behind.

Another where everything is descent.

Another where everything is decrease.

Another whirls in another that whirls in another
that whirls in another that

Another space is completely immobile: its distances
can be established from a single point only.

In another, nothing is fragment. Points are inconceivable,
the same as an isolated line or any segment.

That space is one where nothing straight is possible.

That one where curves do not exist.

The sinuous space where all rectitude is apparent
and where one never meets the shortest path.

The one where concavity is unimaginable.

The one where immobility does not exist
or where one can't tell the difference between
mobile and immobile.

A space where everything moves but nothing is displaced,
or viceversa
or versavice

A spiraling space where alternatively
ascend is descend
or
descend is ascend
but one does not know when.

A space where everything is edge.

An intermittent space.

A space where nothing is full
and where nothing is empty.

Or a space of uniform consistency.

A space where everything is a continuous body.

A space of completely homogenous light.

A dark, empty, limitless space.

So Then

so then I was not dragged along by a whirlwind
through a desert of sand

two armed men did not carry me down a corridor
where all the doors were shut

I did not go on falling interminably

was not brought back to a dinner table where my
father sat silent gazing at us hostile despairing

did not lie in a stupor while voracious ants gnawed
at my belly

did not wait at a border crossing while the guards
searched for my name

did not float unconscious over a greasy sea

did not have to justify myself before those strangers

was not buried by a mudslide

did not wander through that suburban wasteland
looking for something warm from somebody

did not lose my voice in front of the crowded hall

did not go back to the place where nobody recognized me

did not convalesce in a sticky bed

nobody made me remember what I did on the afternoon of a day long ago

they did not shut me up in a black box

I did not search through incessant lists looking for my son

they did not erase my face

my heart did not beat laboriously it did not stop

I come back to the light

day breaks

The Game of the World

The game presupposes all the senses that are attributed to the world. The game of the world requires the joining together of all possible totalities. All partiality is put aside: no particular genre can intervene.

Only the largest groupings are operative. The game consists of combining them in order to produce signifieds that might equal or surpass them.

One has to assemble as much as possible with the conviction that every accumulation is incomplete, contingent, fugitive juncture.

Everything is relevant to the game of the world, but none of its parts involves the whole. No matter how great the expanse, no part is identifiable as world.

If unity and identity correspond to the whole (assuming them to be proper to it), none of the parts possesses them and the difference between the parts turns out to be insignificant. If what is important is the grouping, all separation becomes provisional. All separation arises from circumstantial tactics.

The world is not the game of the world. The game of the world resembles it. The world is not game, but the game offers the only possibility of grasping the world as a continuous unfolding. Game: figuration that mimics what is inimitable. The inimitable is the world, indifferent to the game.

One plays the game of the world in hopes of shaping whatever is heap, mixture, or change, with the desire that the game unfold as world or the contrary, that the world unfold as game.

In the game of the world the game plays more than the world.

Playing the game of the world ends not by seizing the world but by ruining the game.

Playing the game of the world is the most ambitious game one can play and, as such, is interminable.

To play the game of the world one has to play in the world. There is no place outside the world where one can play the game of the world. When we stop playing the game of the world, we are still in the world. But if we cannot leave the world, can we perhaps stop playing the game of the world?

To play the game of the world, one needs conviction.

One needs conviction or ingenuousness, which is the same thing.

Whoever does not play the game of the world, plays without wishing to. It is better to play knowing it, although playing may not be a voluntary act, may be barely an interference.

The world emerges by means of the game of the world. Man generates it at the same time as the latter is engendered by the former.

Every man plays the game of the world according to his skill. Every man recreates the game of the world as his predecessors and successors played it and will play it. The game of the world outlasts all men. The totality of men constitutes the totality of the game of the world, but not the total game.

Without man there is neither world nor game of the world.

Every man assumes his correspondence with the world according to his possibilities. The world shows itself as totality to every man, as different totality. Such differences form part of the game of the world. The game of the world becomes worldwide.

In the game of the world, the participants play without profit. One who wagers in search of gain is not playing the game of the world. In the game of the world there is no winner.

In the game of the world, resolution alternates with thwarting, calm with tempest, prudence with nonsense.

Repetition is inevitable. The game of the world is based on a repetition by turns broken and begun again.

Subject to constant change, the game of the world endures. Other games form part of the game of the world; those that respond to a name make up the unnameable game.

Everything that happens happens to the game of the world. Also the postponed, the concealed, the suspended, what silence hatches belongs to the game of the world.

The game of the world plays with what is uncovered and what is hidden, with the full and with the empty.

The game of the world has a propensity toward intricacy, mazes, tends toward the profuse and the tangled. To play the game of the world is to play at aberrancy.

Advice Column

I am fifty years old, I am an artist. I wanted to be a success, I felt trustful. Little by little, from one fiasco to another, I began losing my self-confidence. Now I feel useless, empty, apathetic, even though I know I have talent, that I am better than many others who are more famous. I never could adapt myself to the rules of the game, to the social hypocrisy, make the concessions necessary to get ahead. My fiascos upset me, make me depressed, my dissatisfaction prevents me from enjoying life. I must tell you that the therapist was able to do very little. Some people suggest a psychoanalyst.
    What shall I do?

Your case is not unique, I will go so far as to say it is common. You magnify your problems, attach too much importance to yourself, or to the immediate results of your work, not to the work itself. Look, the population of the world has surpassed the two thousand million mark; millions barely survive, have almost nothing to eat. Therefore, you are no more than one example of a species already quite remote, which increases progressively, and whose survival, after all, is limited. The universe is contracting, the earth is growing cold. Perhaps one day humans can emigrate to a planet closer to the sun; perhaps they will live as long as the solar system, which in any case is not eternal either; it is also possible that at any moment everything could disappear. If we consider that mental energy is one of the vibrations of matter, think that your ponderings represent hardly more than an infinitesimal movement, like the tiny agitation of a grain of sand in an immeasurable desert. Don't be so egotistical. Your life span is too instantaneous. It's not worthwhile to keep tormenting yourself. In terms of real time, cosmic time, you do not exist.

Something Gives Him Away

Something gives him away: the simulacrum never manages to be entirely complete. To keep it from deceiving us, God prohibited Satan from appearing totally identical to man. His feet, for example, couldn't be shaped the same as ours. (Feet, in the mystical sense, are allegories for sensual passions. Bare feet enhance the desire for carnal contact. Worshipers take great pleasure in kissing the feet of their idols.) The devil's feet usually point backward. We find them disgusting. The deformity means that, although subject to the Supreme Command, they go contrary to it at the same time, are disrespectful of the harmonious designs of God.

They say the devil adopts goosesteps. Perhaps the goose possesses evil qualities that we are not aware of and that suit the infernal order. Its irritating croak or its urge to splash around in the mud, rooting in search of slimy morsels, link it with the perverse and the filthy, with the world of darkness.

Someone, certainly, among the people we see must be a devil, but it turns out to be difficult to discover him. We should become intimate enough with the suspect until some unmistakable sign reveals him to us, always too late, as devil. Subtle signs can give him away: horny armpits covered by hair, a toothed foreskin or a spiny clitoris, a distinct umbilical floriation, a lacerating thorn behind the ear, a certain conformation and certain consistency of the elbow.

Novella

We agreed to meet at his house. I ring the bell.
No answer. Loud ring. Nobody. Riiing.
Nobody. Riiiiing. Nobody. Riiiiiiiiing:
nobody's here or nobody hears. I put my ear against the door:
some muffled sound like a far-off whispering:
steps? plates? voices? something sounds reverberates.
Perhaps he forgot the appointment. That can't be.
BAM... BAM... BAM (I bang with my fist) wait
PIM... PAM... PUM... POM! (with my foot)
He said the second door on the left (or was it on the right?).
Let's try the second on the right: ring... nobody... ring... nothing (could it be the fourth floor?). This absent-minded guy got the day wrong (or did I mix up the date?). He may even have believed it was at my house (now, at this very instant, he could be ringing the bell of my door). He's deaf. He fainted, he collapsed, he's frothing at the mouth/ foaming/ he's shivering, lying on the floor. They called him out on an emergency. (in that case he would have let me know). Burglars broke in, handcuffed him/ gagged him/ he resisted/ they shot him... bleeding, dragging himself, he doesn't manage to reach the door. He's in the bathroom with diarrhea, with cramps (from the bathroom you can't hear worth a damn). He left the gas open (it has no odor). He was taken prisoner, incommunicado/ they are torturing him/ he doesn't survive/ his heart is kaput.

He couldn't stand living anymore because of/ too much frustration/ he is lying on the tiles of the patio. He took sleeping pills/ went to sleep in a steaming hot bath.

He went crazy. He's singing naked, singing naked swaying back and forth, he's singing naked swaying back and forth on the edge of the balcony (he's singing "Che farò senza Eurydice").

He's decided never to communicate with his fellow man again because words are insubstantial and deceiving. He's burned all his papers, cut the telephone line, and is sunk in contemplation without commentary. Passively, he hears the doorbell as an accidental thing, like one of those many games of chance not more or less of a novelty than anything else.   He seduced the woman he desired/ dragged her to his bed/ they tremble coupled together.   He got drunk on fiery spirits, he wanted the sun to enter his guts to illuminate him, he's given himself up to incandescent voluptuousness, to flaming delight, to the thousand steel daggers of alcohol, to his tipsy fire sprites, to the ardent realm of the seraphim with six wings (two to cover the sex) and of the virgin (*viragine*) devourers of gluttons. He drank too much ("Mamma, quel vino è generoso" *Cavallería Rusticana*)/ he's sleeping in his vomit.

No. He's opened his veins, he's sitting in a crimson pool ("En fermant les yeux" *Manon*). He's inflicted with pustulant boils, they swell/ break/ all his internal fluids escape. He stepped on a bar of soap and broke his neck. He wounds himself, tears off his flesh in strips: his bones appear. He swallowed a peach pit, he can't expel it/ it won't go/ he turns purple/ explodes. He electrocuted himself with the electric blanket. His nose is swelling up, it is the map of Italy/ it's Africa/ it's a globe of the world natural size: His insides have dried up, calcified, his skin turns to leather and splits open. He disorganizes disorganization (like this: grointaznoi or like this: ai ai orgnztn).   He's grown wings, he's flying over the city, he ascends pale, more diaphanous all the time, all the time more dangerous, he wants to reach the cloud where they sing with harps.   He becomes covered with scales, his spine grows, a crest of hooks runs down his breastbone, his snout gets longer, his eyes bulge out, he becomes lethargic (he turns into a crocodile), all he can think of is sinking his belly into some stinking mud. He knows he's a dream and wakes up the person who's dreaming him so he can be dissipated, he disappears like a balloon punctured by his dreamer: the butterfly that was dreaming him stops dreaming him. He flagellates himself with a hair shirt, mortifies his flesh with red hot pincers, he cuts off his ears, he opens his belly with the zigzag cut of a saber. Up from the sewers comes the cesspool predators, fasten their proboscis to his body, emulsify him and swallow him. The shadows of the house are conjured up and concentrated so he is sunk in total darkness. His body is narrowed and compresses him, everything is reduced to a tiny and incredibly dense cube.   He immolates himself by fire ("Nessun dorma" *Turandot*) to purify the most warprone species of the earth.   Vampire, he vampires the girl on the fifth (inferno) sadomachists her/ sodomizes her/ babylons her/ ninevehs her/ persepolises her/ gomorrahs her/ incubuses her and succubuses her. He grows fangs, they become encrusted in the opposite gum. Scorpions are nesting in his pillow. Poisoned by the amphisbaenian he was devoured by his daughters or the red ants... or the four-legged rooster with spiny wings and serpent's tail (the eighth serpent as a tail) or the gru or the crocota or the lucrocota ... or they tied him up with a chain forged from the lines of the hand, intermittent fog, comet's tail, spikenard's shadow, frightened dove, memory of a bonfire. While he's looking in the mirror, he becomes wrinkled/ his hair turns white/ he crumples/ mummifies/ turns into powder/ damp ashes/ extinct ashes... I hear steps, they're his steps, I see him coming down the stairs. I don't know that I will accept his excuses.

A Gusto

This glutton I know loves long Augustinians in snap sauce, but he says they are the very devil to catch. First he screams at the top of his voice to chase them down, then rips off their clothes. The spine prepared, he puts in this and that, reduced to pap, mashed with pinches of jiffy, and leaves it all incarnated, soaking till dawn. He drowses three carats with fissures. When it is clarified, put in the specific, grasp the keel, and throw the spine into the gulp. It's not easy to attract long Augustinians. You have to throw them virgules and pieces of essential, you have to swindle forcefully until the pack cracks, warbles, goes into the layer house, and the long Augustenant can close the whathisname with one blow. Later they are skewered with a pinnule. And now you add pepper, syrup, guimpe and pimpernel, and capillary them and roast them on a fire of bags, carefully and lovingly, and in a gluttonous spree they are placed in the cheek, then in the throat. And the confiscation laughs and feasts without chiton and without kid, while dancing the fang dance:

        compose cousins with me
        I invite you to this feast
        strongpoint my long Augustinians
        assail in the throat
        grasp the dredge and pickle
        there is no impudent more spruced up
        than a platterful of long Augustinians

to the fang Sí
to the fang No
for this pack of long Augustinians
fills me up
fills me up
Yaaahooooooooo

Trunkiness

In front of me—before and in front of my gaze gazing out—is that oak trunk. Dark cylinder, rough, striated, consistent. It consists of a live mass; like mine, it changes, but unlike mine, it keeps growing. Like my body, the other one shows the marks of its duration; hardened outside, almost stone-like, nevertheless, as with me, nutritious liquids course through it. I stand in front of and confront something, world at one and the same time alien and mine, a strange thing that possesses the same internal force that gives me life but opposite, set aside, like a part of the outside, like an object that objects to me, I also object to the world that encompasses us both, joins us, entwines us: enigma. That trunk is robust, that resistant thing with its existence so distinct from and yet contemporaneous with mine, is placed there guarding its secret condition, veiled from my capacity to comprehend it.

I perceive the imposing trunk and, in some way that I don't understand, I think that the trunk perceives me. Something emanates from the trunk; the effluvium should be reciprocal. Receptive, without insisting on protecting my identity, I welcome it. The trunk comes near me. I try to change my being, to conceive of myself as trunk. Infused by my I, tranfused, the trunk ceases to be object—hurray! hurray!—manages to be me, becomes more and more fellow creature. I imagine that the trunk also achieves some knowledge of the subject that captures it. As I become aware of it, it becomes aware of me; as I grasp it, it grasps me.

A certain zone of cognition is established between the trunk and me. And within this field there is an interchange between my humanness and its trunkiness; you my I, I your you. Thus we reach a point where I trunkify myself and it humanizes itself, humanness and trunkiness now confounded. I pass it my sameness, it gives me its gistness: ness for ness.

Soon I woodify myself, I consist of cylindrical circles and sap runs through my veins and I feel an irresistible urge to ascend and spread out, I long for humidity, also my feet branch and take root, my body stiffens, my arms knot, I open my hands, my toes sprout, their pulp fills with shoots, my nails turn green and soften and bud. I vegetate.

I long to be fixed, to root in this soil, plant myself with all my strength, stay anchored forever. And at the same time, does the trunk throb? does it become heated? does the blood rush to its head? does it generate an incipient image of what I am, in its sort of fancy? does it manage to take notice of my I, it is of concern to me, does it grant me any existence?

The trunk remains impassive, as if my trunky solidarity didn't affect it at all. Trunk, oh Trunk, if you don't humanize yourself I remain cloistered in myself, with my inmost being closed, all alone with the analogue, with no bridge, limited to fantasizing about the other, to figure myself as what I am not, the unreachable.

Story

This is my story. At last. It's not different from others', I am not different from others, but I got hold of this particular story. In this one I am the principal character.

I wander about, pondering, passing the time.

Now I go out, stroll around, sit down on a bench in the square, watch what's going on.

I think extraordinary things, but they don't happen.

Later I feel hungry. I ought to wait.

My desires change.

I do the same as always.

It's my story. While I can, I hold on to it, expand it. I never had such an opportunity before. I don't want to let it get away.

Things happen, various things happen.

I find it's not worth the trouble to give the details. I don't know about putting someone else in. I don't want to share my story.

The Goal

As usual, at this hour, the worst, the expressway is jam-packed. Today worse than ever. Deluge, I can barely see the car in front of me. The wipers can't keep the windshield clear. Celestial seas hurl themselves, totally pour themselves out over this scrap of earth. Why—I ask myself—did you leave your warm corner? Why did you exchange the pleasant rites of evening—some pleasant music, a glass of wine, in anticipation of a tasty supper—for this dubious suburban adventure? You blockhead, why challenge such inclemency, flinging yourself stupidly into this watery event? Lunatic electron, criptosuicidal one, where do you get this stubborn streak, you collector of calamities. We are wandering, my wife and I (she delighted to go out, no matter where) through the northern outskirts, through places prefigured, yet completely strange, not knowing how to reach our destination. Blackened facades, fading lights, we venture into the inhospitable monotony and end up getting lost. We ask; they give us vague directions, we start out, then backtrack, until at last we find our theater. There are still some people in the lobby. Stragglers, like us. They put us in the front row, but all the way on the side. Thanks to bribes and insistence, they move us to the center. Fortunately the performance is late in starting. The audience is restless, people make a racket; you hear footsteps, greetings, laughing, cellophane being ripped open and crumpled, trumpeting of noses being blown, throats being cleared, coughing, hubbub—all from this kettle of fish. I try to read the program—I know absolutely nothing about what I came to see. One by one the lights go out until everything is in total darkness. At the same time the uproar dies down to a soft whisper, finally ceases. The world starts to vanish, disappears. We remain suspended in the penumbra. Closure with promise of aperture, the interval swells, overflows with anticipation, foretells a thousand and one chimeras. Pregnant prelude, potent with hope. I find my peace, give myself over to this goal more and more expansive, invitation of wide welcome. The soul is softened, ready to receive its desired guests, receptive and open like the front of the stage. The curtain is drawn: the shadow deepens. From the depths of the darkness, a rumor approaches. Cohort of murmuring specters chorus a lugubrious litany, they emerge from a far-off sea, from a recondite, remote gyre: the stage brightens and the cowled characters uncover themselves: change masks. Courtesans, adventurers, buffoons, a magician with two servants—one all breeze, the other all ballast—ghost and freak are presented. They speak with eloquence, discuss, explain, clamor, vociferate. They agree and disagree; affection and disaffection motivate them. Soon a plot is hatched. Soon an intricate story is put into motion so that this pretend family can go about its affairs. Errands, demands, caprices, bustles follow one after the other. We all play the equivocal game. It is decided by the one who, by knotting together events and entwining chances, thus delineates every destiny and links the destinies together. The play works out, is fulfilled, thrills. And yet I long for that first silence, premonitory penumbra, the one that anticipates.

Fickle-Hearted Reader

He goes by the letter, his perpetual embryo, his rambling analogue, his scaler and hurler, his talisman. By the letter he goes and is expanded, sees the vastness. Sees what he couldn't see without this going; what is not given him is given him only by this giver, this repetitious and enfiladed intercessor. Many lives he lives, in his fashion, calls at unknown ports, reaches the palace whose door is the horizon and passes through to the other side, where every road enchants. Letter the projector, he the projectile. He eats forbidden fruit and, like the monkey grammarian, climbs the tree of knowledge. Along with the camel he passes through the eye of the needle, or becomes the eye, the only eye, eye of the Cyclops: emulator of the brightest star, he is. The powers he seeks he finds, at least, by means of a go-between.

When he is not reading, this drab blanket covers him, these walls enclose him, on this oilcloth he eats his grub; he should live his life, his selfsame life. Small world with people who belittle him, who say to him, hit the dirt, first and foremost the gullet, watch your step, a fish in hand, how to make it to the end of the month without a moneylender, your shoe is untied, you must show proof, this seat is taken, be careful with your lumbago. And the poor thing shrivels and shrinks when he's not reading, when he's not reading.

And by reading the subdued one dives in, pledging to bury himself. He takes the track of letters. Letter after letter after letter ... and along the way the narrow path widens. He soars, dives, is metamorphosed: swashbuckler, clever detective, ravisher of Persephone, spy, king of the elves, Cythera, Laputa, Juvencia, Treasure Island: in his goings nobody hinders him. He drinks from every fountain, carries a ring of master keys that offer him codes and arcana. He celebrates feasts with black bold typefaces and small caps; if he's looking for an orgy, he finds one; if he desires beatitude, that too. Fancy, he fancies that he lacks for nothing.

With time, the illusion is dispelled. Pretend as much as you like, this deal is shown to be just what it is: a theater of shadows. Only pipe dreams, air, nothing. The simulacrum flattens out like the page on which it is written. This factory of dreams is less alluring than the window. The reader raises his eyes. Looks out. Busy people going by, people of flesh and blood, clamorous children, tangible beauties. Trees in bloom, birds flying. Activities, attitudes sizzle with fleeting stories. Face to face with the spurs of so many real things, the wonder of fantasy dims, like the letters that transcribe it.

The reader closes the book and goes out into the world. There he goes—don't they see him?—tasting every sensation. Every object takes on a complete, full presence. A pear with carnal rumps, what delight! The titillating spider web sparkles. The sun's glare turns clay shards into diamonds. Reds flare in the carnation. What pleasure to see each form in clear outline. The hand palpates each separate skin, tests each separate firmness. At last, the certainty to exist, to truly exist!

Stimulation that begins to fade, passing fancy: dailiness demands its dues, slowly imposes its burdens. The repetition wearies, wipes out distinctions. One day resembles another: cycle of clods. A hard struggle to subsist. More sorrows than savors. Trudging down the same path, narrowing to nowhere. Obscure screen. Dust that accumulates and is dispersed. Danger of asphyxiation, don't let yourself be smothered. Against the nothingness, to wipe out the world that erases us, one leap suffices. Yippee! And once again he is rapt in his reading.

Amnesia

I have lost my memory. I don't remember who I am. I don't recall that I've been married for twenty-five years, that I've crammed my house full of personal objects, that I have three children to support and care for every single day, that I must manage my meager salary so it makes ends meet, that despite being cautious I get myself embroiled, become poorer, that I don't know how to keep everything from sending me into confusion, that I have my work and that it demands constant attention and absorbs most of my energies, which I had wanted to dedicate at least in part to satisfying an artistic vocation, apparently not compatible with my obligations, that my friends, like my wife and me myself, grow older, are overcome by ailments, die suddenly in full possession of their mental powers, as just happened to those two, most talented, rather young people, that there's tension on all sides, that with the crisis the situation keeps getting worse, that the danger of war is greater every day, more alarming, that difficulties mount up and satisfactions do not compensate, that I no longer have the necessary ability to concentrate with so much noise, so many complications, so much disorder...

Of all this I remember nothing, neither as a whole or in detail. I have just lost my memory. Without a past, without any idea of a link, nothing that occurs around me affects me now. Looking out at an alien world, that's what I need. Don't insist. I don't recognize you. Let me be, let me enjoy a little of this unexpected peace.

Saúl Yurkievich was born in Argentina in 1931. The author of seventeen volumes of poetry and fifteen volumes of criticism and creative prose, he was for thirty-five years Professor of Latin American literature at the Université de Paris Vincennes. He has also taught at many American universities, including Harvard, Chicago, Columbia, Johns Hopkins, UCLA, Maryland, and Pittsburgh. He lives in Paris, France. This book along with an accompanying poetry volume, *Background Noise*, are the first volumes of Yurkievich's work to appear in English.

Cola Franzen was born in Georgia in 1923. One of her translations in the poetry volume won a Pushcart Prize. Her translation of Jorge Guillén's *Horses in the Air* won the Harold Morton Landon Translation Award from the Academy of American Poets. Her recent translations include Alicia Borinsky's *All Night Movie* and Antonio José Ponte's *Tales from the Cuban Empire*. She lives in Cambridge, Massachusetts.

This book was set in the Sabon and Swiss 721BT typefaces. The text and jacket were printed by Phoenix Color Corp. in Hagerstown, Maryland. Both book and jacket were designed by Robert Wechsler. The author photograph on the back cover is by Pierre Getzler.

Catbird Press was founded in 1987 and specializes in literary fiction and sophisticated humor. For more information about Catbird's books, please visit our website, www.catbirdpress.com.